D0445570

The Ninety Million Dollar Mouse

Also by Francis M. Nevins, Jr.

The 120 Hour Clock

THE NINETY MILLION DOLLAR MOUSE

Francis M. Nevins, Jr.

Walker and Company
New York

All the characters and events portrayed in this story are fictitious.

First published in the United States of America in 1987 by the Walker Publishing Company, Inc.

Published simultaneously in Canada by Thomas Allen & Son, Canada, Limited, Markham, Ontario

Library of Congress Cataloging-in-Publication Data

Nevins, Francis M.
The ninety million dollar mouse.

I. Title.
PS3564.E854N5 1987 813'.54 87-10661
ISBN 0-8027-5683-2

Printed in the United States of America

10 9 8 7 6 5 4 3 2 1

FOR JOHN LUTZ

1

Children of the Unity, hear this in your hearts. In the unity of the Circle is the Fullness. Without the unity of the Circle is the emptiness. Bring therefore the emptiness without the Circle into the Fullness within, until the moment of the Circle shall have come, and within the Circle all that was and is and will be shall rest.

The Last Discourse of Barnabas Drake,
Chapter 6, Exhortation 14

I AND MY fellow New Yorkers woke up that morning in October of 1985 to find the city transformed into a steel-and-glass rain forest. Clammy gray sky, fog hiding the tallest building tops, hard rain slashing down on the pavements. As I looked east across town from the windows of my Central Park South high-rise, the dominant sight was gridlock, the reigning sound a cacophony of bus and truck and taxi horns. Only a lunatic or someone with a job would venture out in that combat zone, and I was neither. I showered, shaved, dressed for loafing, straightened the bedroom, breakfasted on fruit and croissants and three cups of Mysore coffee, and resolved to pass the day with an improving book or two and some rousing music on the stereo system to drown the muffled noises from the street. It was a little before noon when they kidnapped me.

I understate the case when I admit I was unprepared for trouble. The lull between scams had been too long, the last flurry of identity-juggling too many months behind me. When I need to hibernate I resume my role as George Boyd, suave and affluent Manhattanite, but I play the part so well, just as I do with every other persona in my repertory, that after a while I lose the edge that is the breath of life, the antennae go limp, the danger sense atrophies. That is when I am most vulnerable, and I know it. But I need my George Boyd life as I need all my lives, and so I embrace the risk, trusting that if an emergency pops up I will rise to the occasion.

Sometimes the magic doesn't work.

It was just short of noon and the Khachaturian Third Symphony was blasting through the quad system into my earphones when I thought I heard a noise from the condo foyer that wasn't in the orchestral score. I swung out of the recliner chair with the earphones still on me, and what did my wondering eyes behold but two men whom I'd never seen before in my life, stepping gingerly into my living room. The one in the lead was a white-haired and wrinkled little gnome, beaming benevolently through cheap plastic-rimmed glasses, a tan leather attaché case in one hand. The other guy could have been a pro basketball star, six and a half feet high, chocolate-skinned and rangy and sporting a close-cropped mustache and beard. He was the one with the .357 Magnum pointed at me.

For a microsecond I thought he was going to kill me, that I was about to be splattered all over my condo, for no reason in the world that I knew of, and with the funereal organ solo from the Khachaturian Third as my sign-off theme. The terror that went through me for that split second is beyond human power to put into words.

Then I noticed that the black guy wasn't aiming the Mag at me anymore. He was holding it loose and relaxed, with the barrel pointing down at the Karastan. And there was a big friendly grin in the man's eyes that didn't look at all like the smile of an assassin. Meanwhile the old gnome had set down the attaché case on my coffee table and had gone down on one knee and was twiddling the combination dials set into the leather surface. Then he took a key from a ring in his pocket and unsnapped one of the twin locks, and took a second key from another pocket and unsnapped the other. With a mischievous twinkle in his eyes he flung open the attaché case and spun it on the table so its contents faced me.

Its contents was money. Ten neat crisp sheaves of twenties. The gnome nodded at me, and I leaned over and extracted one of the sheaves and riffled it. Fifty twenties in the sheaf. As far as I could tell from some split-second tests they were not counterfeit.

The gnome reached into a hip pocket and pulled out a matching tan leather cardcase from which, with a smile and a headwaiter's bow, he drew a card and laid it atop one of the sheaves of bills still in the attaché case. I forced myself to withdraw attention from the thousand dollars' worth of twenties in my hand and glance down at the card. The printing was in raised gold letters on heavy bond: OMNITRON TECHNOLOGIES, INC., *Ewan P. McGaughy, Director of Research*.

"It's pronounced McGuffy," the gnome said. "Mr. Turner, it's a great pleasure to meet you." He held out a tiny hand dimpled with age spots.

At first I didn't think I'd heard him right, and then I knew I had and fought like a tiger to keep a poker face and make a stab at preserving my identity. "My name," I told him with a dignity not quite in keeping with the situation, "is George Boyd. Whoever you are, I'm afraid you've broken into the wrong unit."

"Your name," he smiled back at me without malice, "is Milo Turner. You have a rather impressive number of other names but Turner is, how shall I put it, the substratum, the foundation."

"It is not," I insisted, while inside I was screaming to myself, *How does he know?*

"Yes, it is, Mr. Turner, but I do understand your hesitation in admitting it to a total stranger so I shan't press you. By the way, the gentleman with me is Dave Landy, my right hand."

"Pleasure," the beanpole grunted, his eyes still beaming that amiable hi-neighbor look.

"Dave takes me just about anywhere in this world I want to go. I'm afraid the security system in your building is far from flawless, Mr. Turner."

"Mr. Boyd," I corrected. "I'll have to take that problem up with the management committee. But I don't think you broke in here to try to sell burglar alarms. If this money is meant for me, then it's the other way around, there's something of mine you want to buy."

"Just an afternoon and evening of your time," McGaughy said. "Mr Turner—"

"Mr. Boyd," I insisted.

"—We want to have a conference with you at our world headquarters, in south central Jersey. In this rain the drive will take two hours, more or less, but you'll be most comfortable all the way. You will be treated to a gourmet lunch on wheels and a, well, a sort of sneak preview of the situation. After the conference you'll be free to accept the offer that will be made to you or to turn it down. Either way, the contents of the attaché case are yours for your time and trouble, plus you can keep the case. You will be home before midnight. Satisfactory?"

"Puzzling," I said, "but okay, I'll ride with you."

I did insist however that we first make a pit stop at my bank, six blocks from Central Park South, so I could stow the ten thousand in my George Boyd safe-deposit box. If I left the money in the condo, why couldn't McGaughy and his black angel ease their way in a second time and take back the cash while I was in conference? Just in case this turned out to be an elaborate buildup to my own execution, which was a remote but real possibility, I also tossed into the deposit box a quickly scrawled note to the police, with McGaughy's business card attached.

By one in the afternoon I was luxuriating in the vast rear compartment of a silver-gray Cadillac stretch limo, while Landy, behind the wheel and in chauffeur's cap, maneuvered us through the dingy cityscape. We slid uptown with radials hissing against the soaked pavement, crossed to Jersey on the GW, and rode I-80 to the junction with the turnpike, at which point we headed south. One after another of the dismal communities of north Jersey evaporated into the gray gloom behind us. The ride was so smooth I felt as if I were sitting still, in some museum of architectural history, watching a panorama streak by my viewing port.

Once on the turnpike, McGaughy touched a button in the armrest on his side and a small but sturdy table sprang up from the floorboards between us. He unlocked a compartment built into the base of the jump seats, and within two minutes the table was set with flatware on a crisp linen cloth. McGaughy decanted seafood-pasta salad from a covered bowl onto our plates and poured Pouilly Fuissé into chilled glasses. Afterward came a pair of obscenely rich napoleons, and steaming coffee from a unit built into the back of the front seat, and Grand Marnier. I marveled at what a customized limo could be made to disgorge, I savored every morsel and drop, but mainly I listened. The subject of McGaughy's luncheon discourse was religion.

"How much do you know," he began, "about the Drakean Union?"

I let the wine go down smooth and slow to give myself time to think. "About as much as I know about Islam or Christian Science or Taoism," I said. "Just a little. Bits and pieces I've picked up from *Time* and *Newsweek* or whatever. Any reason why you care?"

"I don't want to waste our time telling you what you already know. Well, as you're probably aware, the Drakean Union was founded in the late nineteenth century by Barnabas Drake, the great railroad tycoon and, well, robber baron. In his younger years he had made a gargantuan fortune out West and had destroyed untold numbers of other people to do it. Small farmers, homesteaders, Indian tribes, whatever stood in his way, he cut down. He owned a lot of lawmakers, so a great deal of his butchery was technically legal. If it wasn't, he did it anyway."

"Like the Bitterroot Massacre?"

"No, that was strictly legal, even though it made his name a symbol around the world for, well, for what the name Hitler stands for around most of the world today. He used his connections with the military to instigate the worst massacre in American history. More than seventeen hundred Indian men, women, and children were slaughtered by the cavalry during four bloody days and nights in the summer of 1877. Afterward he bought up their reservation land for five cents on the dollar and built another railroad through their burial ground. That was Barnabas Drake."

"It was until the Event," I said. "Isn't that the Drakeans' name for it?"

"Precisely. The Event. Drake's writings never revealed just what this Event was. He would never speak or write about it afterward except in highly figurative language. Some Drakeans think it was what today we call an out-of-body experience that he supposedly underwent at a moment of near death. Others claim it was a form of contact with the supernatural. The Drakean Christians think he saw Jesus. Whatever it was, it changed his life utterly and forever. He liquidated everything he owned, turned it over to a foundation he organized, and spent the rest of his life traveling, teaching, and writing. His collected works run to over seventy thick volumes. He died at the age of eighty-three, in 1905. Today the Drakeans claim forty million members worldwide, perhaps seven million here in the States. The Union controls a publishing house, a cable network, and its members are in most of the power-wielding professions. Barnabas Drake University is ranked with the finest institutions of higher learning in the country. There are at least four Drakeans in the Senate and twenty-five or thirty in the House. Doctors, lawyers, movie and rock stars, businessmen, educators, labor leaders—there are Drakeans everywhere you turn."

"From your tone," I said, "I might almost believe I'm lunching with one."

"Oh, goodness no!" he spluttered, and coughed as a bit of pasta went down the wrong pipe. "I don't have a religious bone in my body! Neither do most of the people you'll meet in an hour or so." He patted his pale lips gently with a silk handkerchief. "Although I've always suspected Bob Fest of being a secret Presbyterian. . . . No, the reason I've been lecturing about the Drakean Union is quite simple. We believe that the Drakeans are planning to take over Omnitron. We want you to help us fight them off."

"Ah," I said in the tone of one who suddenly sees light. "So you've got a corporate raider on your back, is that it?"

"Far from it. The Drakeans haven't bought a share of our stock, as far as I know, and they aren't likely to in the future. If the courts uphold their claim, they won't need to. They'll own us without having had to pay out a cent. Except for lawyers of course."

I bought another few seconds of thinking time by lingering over the last swallow of liqueur. How could they legally take over a hugely successful high-tech corporation without . . . And then the connections fused together in my head and I remembered. Omnitron Technologies. What was the name of the whiz kid who'd started the company? Kilby, that was it, Charles Kilby. Boy wonder of the computer chip. Founded Omnitron at age twenty, made the Fortune 500 by twenty-three, died of a massive coronary in one of the corporate Lear jets at thirty-four, fourteen or fifteen months ago. I had been in Stockholm at the time, lecturing to the national police academy in my persona as Professor Dr. Horst Gerstad, the eminent German criminologist, and had been neglecting to read the U.S. newspapers. But the death of Charles Kilby was news around the world. I couldn't recall that he'd been a Drakean.

As if he had been reading my mind, McGaughy broke in on my train of thought. "I take it," he said, "you haven't been following the saga of Chuck's two wills and the brouhaha over his legal domicile. I'm not surprised you haven't. The network news programs won't cover it because it's too complicated and doesn't have any glitzy visuals. Even the piece on it in the *Times* was oversimplified. Well, we have a law professor waiting to brief you on that aspect of the situation." He swiveled his birdlike head away from me and slid over on the velour seat cushions to peer out the side window's tinted glass. "Another twenty minutes."

"I can hardly wait," I mumbled.

"One question of etiquette." McGaughy cleared his throat with a delicate little cough. "I take it you still insist you are not Milo Turner and have never heard of the fellow?"

"I am *not* Milo Turner!" I allowed just the right touch of anger and indignation to flavor the words. "You gave ten thousand dollars to the wrong man. Haven't I been telling you that since the minute you and Landy broke in on me?"

"Of course you have, of course you have. And we're all gentlemen at Omnitron so naturally we'll take you at your word. However"—another gentle cough—"however, we at Omnitron don't have a shred of interest in the fellow who calls himself George Boyd. The person we are interested in is the well-known if sometimes hard-to-find private investigator, Arthur Lattman." Pause for effect. "Of course, you're not that man either, are you?"

He had me. God, he had me twice. *How could he know?* I swallowed the brassy taste of fear in my mouth and tried to keep my face on straight.

"But you can fake it, I'm sure. As far as everyone else you'll meet is concerned, you are Lattman. Once we leave this vehicle the names Turner and Boyd will not be pronounced. Fair enough?"

"No complaint from this corner," I answered too quickly. If McGaughy or Landy or the limo itself was wearing a wire, I thought, and if our dialogue ever got heard by the wrong ears, my lives were over.

And the old rascal beamed on me like the elf in a fairy tale, reopened the food compartment and checked to make sure a serving of everything was left—"Dave hasn't eaten yet," he said—and settled back in the cushions. He shut his eyes, and catnapped until the limousine swung off Route 1 and under a gleaming square-cornered steel archway and along the freshly macadamized private drive that led to our corporate destination.

2

We learn that the Law is higher than all other sciences from the fact that he who is learned in the Law finds it easy to understand any other science, but he who has learned other sciences finds it difficult to understand the Law.

Rabbi Pinchas of Koretz, *Nofeth Tzufim*

New Jersey used to be the place you had to go through to get somewhere else. Manhattanites made jokes about the cranberry bogs and the pollution stink and the suburban palaces of mafiosi. Nowadays they don't tell Jersey jokes, or if they do their laughter is edged with nervousness. Atlantic City sucked away millions in gambling business from Las Vegas, the Meadowlands stadiums brought big-time sports and entertainment into what had been swamps, the decaying old cities along the left bank of the Hudson, like Jersey City and Union City and Hoboken, started to attract thousands of businesses and tens of thousands of residents sick of the crime and corruption and filth and ripoffs in what is laughingly called the Big Apple. Economically New York and New Jersey are at war, and Jersey's winning. Someday I may have to move there and set up an identity.

A few years back, the panjandrums of high technology discovered the twenty-six-mile segment of Route 1 that runs between New Brunswick and Princeton, and transformed a boresome stretch of nothing into the Xanadu East of the microchip. Amid the sprawl of companies with vaguely science-fictional names stood the seventeen-story tower of steel and glass that was the world headquarters of Omnitron Technologies, on whose roof I stood at three-thirty that gloomy afternoon, encased in a slim phallic Plexiglass cylinder, looking out and up and around at a charcoal-sketch panorama of lowering clouds and functional architecture, and congested parking lots and the headlights of trucks, buses, and autos crisscrossing on the network of highways I could see from my futuristic conning tower.

So here I am, I thought, but where the hell am I?

I heard shoes clunking on the enclosed spiral stairs that led to the observation post, and the next moment McGaughy was beside me, watching me watch the view. "You ought to see it late at night," he said. "Chuck loved this place. When he'd been working late here and couldn't sleep, he'd lug a chair from his suite with him and sit and stare for hours. Once he made up a little poem about it. 'I love the symphony of light that plays upon the face of night.' I'm afraid that's all I remember."

"You said a chair from his suite? You mean he lived here in the building?"

"When he stayed in Jersey, yes. There are four very nice suites on the executive floor. One was reserved for him at all times—Dave has a key to it now—and two are for business guests."

"And the fourth?"

"Mine," he said. "I came up to tell you that we'll be ready in a few minutes. Dave is setting up the projection room. And I thought I'd say a few words about the people you'll be meeting after the films."

"That would be nice," I said, which was a classic of understatement, since I was beginning to feel as if I'd been whisked off into outer space by extraterrestrials.

McGaughy cleared his throat in that special noisy way that signifies the start of a memorized spiel. "Omnitron," he said with more than a tinge of pride, "is the third most successful high-tech corporation east of the Mississippi. Annual sales are now in the high twelve-figure range, net profits around ninety million a year. Our secret is diversification. We're firmly entrenched in all significant aspects of the market. Weapons-design computers for the military, miniaturized video cameras for police surveillances, mainframe units for thousands of business needs, random-access memory semiconductor chips, lap computers, electronic translators that can take any document you type on a keyboard in one language, say Japanese, and convert it into audiotape in English or German. Our latest offering is an electronic monitor that we're selling to thousands of cities as a cheap alternative to sending nonviolent criminals to prison. The monitor sounds an alarm in the probation office if the person it's attached to strays more than 150 feet from his or her telephone. We are one of the few major American high-techs that compete effectively with the Japanese. We have satellite headquarters in Delaware, in Houston, and of course in California—Silicon Valley. We employ more than twelve thousand people all told. Here, take this." He unbuttoned his threadbare suit jacket and, with the air of a magician producing a bunny, plucked out a glossy brochure. I wondered if he kept it there regularly, the way street people wear old newspapers next to their skin for warmth. Its front cover read *Omnitron* in futuristic lettering and *Annual Report 1984* in more conventional characters, with a computergraphic rendition of the building in which we stood filling the rest of the cover space. I flipped through the pages of corporate self-congratulations and accountants' statements and hoped that no one would expect me to become knowledgeable about this garbage.

"Turn to the section marked Personnel, if you will," McGaughy suggested. I did, and saw that most of it consisted of multicolored charts, and gave the white-haired imp a look of puzzlement. "The pages headed Board of Directors and Senior Management," he said. I riffled through the section and found them.

The names and titles and photographs told me that both the board and the senior management team consisted of the same quartet. The man who was president, chief executive officer, and chairman of the board of directors was a tall, Lincoln-lean, silver-haired character whose name was given as Whitfield J. Shaw, Col., USMC, Ret. He looked mean and gaunt enough to be a retired Marine colonel too, except for one touch, a beautifully shaped spade beard that made him look more like a Castilian grandee. "You will definitely be meeting the colonel," McGaughy promised me.

The rest of the poohbahs on the glossy page of the brochure came across to the camera's eye as creatures of lower rank. A dark-mopped double-chinned young man with heavy five o'clock shadow was identified as Martin Genetelli, vice-president for legal affairs and secretary of the board of directors. A ginger-haired gargoyle with popeyes and a toad face was Robert A. Fest, vice-president for finance and secretary of the board. The vice-president for administration, who had no title on the board except simply Director, was a fortyish nerd with bifocals named Herbert Vanderwell.

"I don't know how many of the other senior managers will sit in with us," McGaughy said. "I do know one in that brochure who will not, and that's Marty Genetelli."

"The head of your legal department isn't going to sit in on a problem with all sorts of legal ramifications?"

"The head of our legal department *is* going to sit in. But Genetelli doesn't hold that position any more. That's another aspect of your assignment."

I pursed my lips in a silent whistle as I felt the plot thickening around my ankles.

"The screening room should be ready by now," McGaughy said, and made a move to go down the spiral stairs.

"Just one question," I stopped him. "Why isn't your name and mug shot in this brochure, McGaughy? Don't you count as senior management?"

"Oh, good heavens, no!" His chuckle of impish glee bubbled up from his checker-vested midsection. "I'm a mere department head, the humblest munchkin in this entrepreneurial Oz."

Some munchkin, I thought. A genial little gnome who could propose me for this assignment, whatever it was, penetrate at least two of my firmest identities, catch me napping, whisk me off to central Jersey, and introduce me to the colonel and the rest of the corporate brass as one of my own cover personalities. I had much to learn about Omnitron, but on one point I was already dead certain. Its extravagant brochure didn't begin to reflect the real flow of power in this outfit.

"Come now," McGaughy said, beckoning me to follow him down the corkscrew stairs. "We have a film festival for your pleasure."

We went along the richly carpeted corridor of the executive floor to a sealed doorway, which slid open for us when McGaughy tapped some sort of signal on a green square set in the teak-paneled wall. I let him lead me down a gentle incline to the front of a fully equipped screening room of the sort that all the studios maintained back in the golden days of Hollywood. The room was empty except for a tall and statuesque black woman in the front row, who was dressed in a severely tailored power ensemble of dark blue skirt and jacket and a tie with a white silk blouse. She rose from the upholstered blue armchair as McGaughy brought me over for introductions.

"Mr. Lattman, I'd like you to meet La Verne De Nise Nixon-Markson, our VP for legal affairs and secretary of the board of directors. La Verne, this is Mr. Lattman, the private investigator."

"Delighted," she murmured in a deep husky voice, and gave me a thousand-watt smile of dignified welcome."

"Likewise," I said, taking her offered hand. "So you're filling what used to be Mr. Genetelli's position, right?"

"I see Ewan has been prepping you," she said. "I haven't been with Omnitron but nine months so I thought I'd take in the movies with you, and then introduce you to Professor Donovan, who's got a lot of law to bring you up to date on." She spoke very slowly and distinctly, as if constantly in fear that she'd slip into an unbusinesslike locution. In affirmative action parlance she was a twofer, a person whose presence gave a company plus marks on both the race quota and the sex quota. She was obviously quite young and not yet at home in the rarefied air of corporate management, and I could understand why she might welcome a law professor as an outside consultant on this messy legal problem I was about to find dumped in my lap.

"It will be a pleasure," I said, and took a seat at her left as McGaughy slipped past us into an armchair on the other side of her and lifted his hand toward the projection booth in a Go signal. The room lights went low and a blinding-bright rectangle formed on the screen and the show began.

First on the bill was a cinematic gem entitled "Omnitron: Making the Future." It was a slick corporate promo, fifteen to twenty minutes long, designed for conventions and trade shows, full of glitzy eye-dazzling rock-video effects. Its purpose was to introduce the viewer to the company, with brief recaps of how it was founded, how it had influenced the technology of today, how it was working even now to shape the technology of tomorrow. Much of it was over my head, high-tech ignoramus that I am, but I did catch a passing remark of the narrator's that all of Omnitron's stock was privately owned and not traded on the exchanges. In the few brief shots of the management team at work I recognized the anorexic hidalgo in the cashmere suit as Colonel Shaw but couldn't identify any of the others: poor cinematography.

Next came another miniature epic with the pretentious title "Kilby: The Dream and the Man." This was a solemn little rehash of the life and achievements of Charles Brockden Kilby, born in a dreary burg in western Illinois, self-taught in the rudiments of computer science, miraculously endowed with the ability to dream up uses for the new technology and to create the technology which would make those uses come alive. The picture celebrated this visionary workaholic who never married, never had a serious relationship with any other person, and who reaped the rewards that the free enterprise system offers for such dedication: he was a multimillionaire in his middle twenties, had graced the covers of *Time* and *Newsweek* three times each before his thirtieth birthday, had etched his name indelibly in the fabric of the way we live. (That is a direct quote from the picture.) Pseudo–John Williams music bursting with victorious pride filled the soundtrack as the narrator recited the litany of inventions that were the direct fruit of Kilby's genius. Somehow the filmmakers never got around to telling us that their hero had died of a coronary at age thirty-four after making do for years on three to four hours of sleep a night. "The picture was finished six months before Chuck died," McGaughy whispered to

Ms. Nixon-Markson and me. "We've never shown it since."

The closing credits trailed off the screen, the rectangle of brightness went dark, the room lights came up, and we blinked. "Good show," I murmured politely. "What happens next?"

"Now," McGaughy said, "I introduce you to the people who will explain why you're here. La Verne, you'll want to attend the meeting, right?"

"If you'd like me to," she replied meekly, which again gave me furiously to wonder about the real chain of command in this outfit where the VP for Legal Affairs was so deferential to a munchkin. We rose and slithered crabwise to the end of the aisle and allowed McGaughy to lead us back into the teak-paneled corridor and along a passageway to a door labeled *Executive Conference Room,* which he opened without knocking. Three men in power suits and one in a rumpled combo of slacks and tweedy sport jacket were congregated around a portable bar in the corner. McGaughy led our group over to the quartet and cleared his throat. "Mr. Lattman," he said, "I'd like you to meet our CEO, Colonel Shaw. Colonel, Arthur Lattman, the finest private investigator in the business."

"Pleasure." The lanky grandee transferred his pipe to his left hand and thrust out his right like a weapon. "Ewan's given you quite a buildup, Lattman. I hope he hasn't been kidding us." With a curt dip of his head he signaled for the rest of the crew to come forward and be introduced.

"Bob Fest, our VPF." The shot of him in Omnitron's brochure had done him full justice. His eyes bulged, his thin ginger hair needed a comb, and overall he bore a distinct resemblance to a swamp toad. The hand he offered me was moist and limp. He kept darting glances around the conference room as if looking for bugs.

"Herb Vanderwell, our VPA." Thanks to Shaw's gesture, I identified the bifocaled nerd as Omnitron's Vice President for Administration. The photo I'd seen of him didn't help. He was one of those colorless supernumeraries who drift out of one's memory three seconds after they wander in. "And this," Shaw said finally, "is Professor Donovan, on leave from Rutgers Law School. We've hired him away from academe for a while to represent Omnitron in this mess."

"Aaron Donovan," the rumpled scholar piped. Cross Groucho Marx with an owl and Donovan would be the result. Underweight, hair skimpy on top, thick mustache, dark-rimmed glasses, slightly bent-over posture. "I've read some Hammett and Chandler but you're my first PI in the real world."

"However," McGaughy said, "today you're the professor's student, Mr. Lattman. I believe he has a little lecture for you. Right?"

"If everyone's ready," Colonel Shaw rumbled, which was the signal for us newcomers to make drinks if we wished and adjourn to the boat-shaped conference table that dominated the room. I settled for black coffee and La Verne Nixon-Markson for a diet cola, which McGaughy dispensed with a twinkle. Apparently he wasn't thirsty. He took his own seat at the table empty-handed. As the herd instinct would have it, the five Omnitron regulars and I bunched together at one end of the table. In front of each of the tan leather chairs was a thick yellow pad in a fancy holder, and precisely aligned with each pad was a gray razorpoint pen. Shaw, Fest, Vanderwell, and Ms. Nixon-Markson uncapped their pens. McGaughy didn't, but the way he leaned toward me suggested that I'd better be prepared to take a lot of notes, so I followed the lead of the majority.

Donovan had slouched down to the far end of the table to where a heap of books and papers and file folders had been piled, but he made no move to sit. He stood facing us, paced back and forth for half a minute like a prisoner in his cell, organizing his thoughts. Then he swung about to face us again and took a deep breath and launched himself.

"Charles Brockden Kilby had a coronary and died in the Omnitron Lear jet fourteen months ago," he began. "He died testate. That means he left a will. One might say he died excessively testate—he left two wills." He paused as if giving us time to clap, or at least to titter politely. No one obliged him. "That's one of the legal problems we face. But there's another problem. The second problem is connected with the wills situation but logically comes before it, so I'll explain this other problem first.

"Mr. Kilby was an incredibly dynamic, incredibly successful entrepreneur. His business interests ranged all over this country and indeed over much of the world. They were all he lived for. He was a restless man and something of a recluse. Very few people saw him on any sort of regular basis. No one knew him well."

McGaughy, sitting at the narrow end of the table at a right angle to me, put his hand to his imp face so his colleagues couldn't see what he was doing and, half-turned toward me, silently mouthed the words: "I did."

"Mr. Kilby had a lot of residences, scattered throughout the United States," Donovan continued, "and indeed had residences also in Mexico and Canada and a few in Europe. But there were no more than seven American residences in which he could be said to have spent substantial time. Our second legal problem is which of these seven residences constitutes his domicile. Mr. Lattman, do you know the legal significance of domicile?"

"Of course he doesn't," Colonel Shaw thundered before I had a chance to open my mouth. "Explain it to him." Long as the conference table was, I could see Professor Donovan flush. Across from me, Ms. Nixon-Markson winced in sympathy with the poor guy. Fest blinked. Vanderwell had nothing on his face at all. Donovan recovered his composure and was back on track in no time.

"Under our system of law," he went on, "there's only one state which is allowed to tax a dead person's estate, and that's the state where the decedent was domiciled at his death. When a decedent is very rich, as indeed Mr. Kilby was, and has divided his time among several homes in several states, as indeed Mr. Kilby did, it sometimes happens that some or all of those states will claim the decedent as its domiciliary, with each one looking of course to take a big tax bite out of his estate." He peered down the table's length in my direction. "Clear so far, Mr. Lattman?"

I looked up from my already well-marked legal pad. "Perfectly clear," I said loudly, in hopes it would make him feel better.

Donovan took time out to pace back and forth a few more seconds. "'When that happens," he resumed, "the decedent's estate faces a huge danger, namely that the courts in each of several states will rule that the dead person was domiciled there, with the result that the estate will indeed be liable for multiple taxation. There are only two ways the estate can prevent this from happening. One way is by persuading the states to compromise and settle the case, with each state getting an agreed-upon fraction of an agreed-upon total sum. The other way is to obtain a judicial decision in one state—preferably one with low estate-tax rates—that can legally bind all the others. Neither of these is terribly easy to do. But if the estate does the wrong thing, or indeed does nothing, it can be literally wiped out by conflicting tax claims." He paused, looked down at the jumble of books and papers in front of him, snatched a file folder out of the heap, opened it, and began to read.

"There was a horrible example of what can happen right here in Jersey," he said, "back in the early 1930s. Dr. Dorrance, the founder of Campbell's Soup, was worth about one hundred fifteen million dollars when he died. In today's money that would make him a billionaire. Dorrance was born in Pennsylvania but moved to western New Jersey when he was thirty and stayed here for many years. By 1925 his daughter was of debutante age, and Dorrance wanted her to have the benefits of Philadelphia social life, so he bought a huge house in Radnor, Pennsylvania, and made that his principal residence. He spent most of his time in Radnor from then on, kept most of his belongings there, and had most of his servants move there. Only a handful were left in Jersey to take care of his house on this side of the Delaware. But he always insisted that he intended to maintain his domicile in Jersey, and any time he had to give his residence on any business or official papers he'd always list the Jersey house. Indeed he even kept up his membership in a Jersey church.

"When he died, Pennsylvania claimed him as its domiciliary and levied a huge inheritance tax on his estate. His executors fought the levy in the Pennsylvania courts and claimed his domicile was Jersey. The Supreme Court of Pennsylvania upheld the levy. The judges wrote a very learned opinion. They held that no matter what you say about your intent to be domiciled in one state, it's your objective acts that count, and when Dorrance set up his principal residence in Pennsylvania, by God that made him a Pennsylvania domiciliary whether he liked or intended it or not.

"But needless to say, that didn't end the matter. Meanwhile the state of New Jersey had *also* claimed Dorrance as a domiciliary and demanded an inheritance tax of something like seventeen million dollars. That levy was appealed to the New Jersey Supreme Court, and that court ruled that Dorrance was indeed a Jersey domiciliary. The judges wrote a very learned opinion. They held that if you have more than one residence, then by God your domicile is the one you *intend* to be your domicile, and Dorrance had said over and over again that he intended to be domiciled in Jersey. Such are the joys of legal reasoning. Are you still with me?"

I wanted to ask Donovan something but couldn't conjure up the words to do it with. It had been too many years since last I'd impersonated a lawyer. "There was no way of . . . well, of . . ." was as far as I could go before I got tongue-tied.

"Getting a judgment by which both Pennsylvania and New Jersey would be bound?" Donovan rescued me. "No way. Once Dorrance's executors argued in Pennsylvania that he was domiciled in New Jersey, they were precluded from arguing in New Jersey that he was domiciled in Pennsylvania. That's a rule we call estoppel. I'll explain it in full detail if you'd like," he said eagerly.

With all the tact I could muster I begged him to do me no favors.

"The only hope the executors had," he went on, inexorably as a steamroller, "was to petition the U.S. Supreme Court to take the case on certiorari. If the court had agreed to hear the matter, its judgment would have been binding on both states."

"But the court refused?"

"Indeed it did. The court won't hear a case of that sort unless the total tax levies of all the states involved exceeds the estate's total value. So Pennsylvania took its bite out of Dorrance's assets over there, and Jersey took its bite out of his assets over here, and his family had to make do with seventy or eighty mil. I bleed for them," Donovan said.

I had been scrawling madly on my legal pad during the professor's lecture, and my wrist was beginning to feel the strain. Gratefully I set down the razorpoint and leaned back in the leather chair. "So," I said. "That, in a nutshell, is the problem Kilby's estate has to deal with, except that you've got seven states trying to tax the property, not just two."

"Correct," Donovan nodded. "But in our case we also have a great advantage over the Dorrance executors' situation. We don't have to worry about conflicting judgments of domicile from different states. Thanks to a different procedural posture we can be sure that ultimately only one state will be held to have been Mr. Kilby's domicile. Tell me, Mr. Lattman, how much civics do you remember from school?"

Strange phrases like unicameral and bicameral legislature raced unbidden along my memory chain. "Not a hell of a lot," I admitted.

"Do you recall that the U.S. Supreme Court has original jurisdiction over suits between or among the states?"

I kept my face blank and hoped that my silence would keep the professor talking.

"In other words," he said, "if a state has a dispute with another state, under the constitution the only court that can hear that dispute is the Supreme Court, which, well, sort of becomes a trial court for that purpose."

A feeble glimmer of enlightenment showed through the legalese murk and I groped for it. "Do I understand that you somehow got the seven states to fight out the case in the Supreme Court instead of each one going through its own court system?"

"Exactly." He beamed down the table at me as if I were a student of scholarship caliber. "And since the Supreme Court doesn't have a trial division or trial facilities, it appointed what is known as a special master to—well, to be the trial judge in the case, reach an initial decision, which eventually the full Court will review—or more likely, just rubber-stamp."

"Nice work if you can get it," I remarked inanely.

"The special master," Donovan said, "is another law professor. George Calamannon, University of Chicago. One of the most respected conflict-of-law scholars in the world."

"Sounds like the case needs an expert," I said. "I imagine the paperwork is enormous."

"My God," Donovan groaned at an obviously painful memory. "With seven states each clamoring for millions in inheritance taxes? Mr. Lattman, I've been assigned one of the office suites in this building, and it has gotten so cluttered with pleadings, interrogatories, requests for admissions, motions, exceptions, briefs, memoranda, and God knows what else that there is literally no room left for me." He coughed, cleared his throat for effect. "Calamannon handed down his ruling two weeks ago. Kilby died domiciled in California. We're playing the game through but we don't expect the full Court to reverse. California's the state whose courts will have to decide which of Mr. Kilby's two wills is the one that counts."

"Well," I said, "where do I come in?"

Colonel Shaw, who had been puffing patiently on his pipe during the legal discourse, stirred in his chair and aimed the pipestem at me. "Donovan's briefing was for background," he snapped, "so you'll understand the big picture." He lifted himself to his feet, and within two seconds Fest and Vanderwell and Nixon-Markson were following the leader and stretching their own legs. McGaughy kept his seat. I stuck with McGaughy.

"Meeting's adjourned," Shaw announced, and tapped his pipe thunderously against the edge of a steel ashtray. "The rest of you are excused. Lattman, you and

McGaughy will meet in the garden in fifteen minutes. La Verne will pull together all the files you'll need and find you a place where you can study them."

"An outdoor meeting," I asked mildly, "in this weather?"

McGaughy treated me to another of those benevolent loon grins. "In this establishment," he said, "the garden is not out of doors. Come, I'll show you the way."

3

Enter the Garden, ye and your wives, to be made glad. Therein are brought round for them trays of gold and goblets, and therein is all that souls desire and eyes find sweet. And ye are immortal therein.

The Koran, 43: 70–71.

I SHOULD HAVE guessed. The place where, after a john break, the conversational threads were picked up was an indoor garden on the order of several I had savored in the lobbies of New York's upscale business towers. It was a huge open space four stories high, extending the length of the building's west side, walled in black marble, choked with hanging plants and ferns and potted trees and exotic greenery, saturated with the peaceful rushing sound of a man-made waterfall, which was supposed to relax the Omnitron honchos and invited guests while they made megabuck talk. As McGaughy and I took seats at a white wrought-iron table, he informed me in a conspiratorial whisper that this was the executive garden and that an employees' garden of the same lushness was parallel to it on the east side of the building. No other executives were enjoying the garden at the moment. The corporation's in-house gnome tented his fingers into a nest for his chin and spoke.

"Chuck Kilby was an extremely wealthy man," he said. "But most of that wealth consisted of one type of asset only. Mr. Turner—pardon me, Mr. Lattman—can you deduce what that was?"

My mind wandered back to that gem of cinematic dazzlement known as "Omnitron: Making the Future" and snatched a shard of fact from the continuity. "All of this company's stock is privately owned," I said. "By Kilby?"

"Smart man," McGaughy chortled. "Yes, roughly two-thirds of Omnitron's stock was in Chuck's name. A great deal of what one might think he owned personally is actually owned by the corporation. That includes homes, limos, planes, furniture . . . Very favorable setup from a tax standpoint, I'm told. The only item of poor Chuck's estate that Omnitron as a corporation gives a damn about is his stock."

"Because whoever owns the stock controls the corporation?"

"Correct."

"And the corporation doesn't want to be controlled by a religion like the Drakean Union?"

"*Especially* not by a religion like the Drakean Union."

"Why not?" I ventured.

"Because it's a chameleon," he said. "Mercurial. Unpredictable. When Barnabas Drake was alive his personality and his writings, well, they held the movement together. Since then there have been so many reinterpretations, so many shifts of doctrine. . . . You can believe in anything, everything, or nothing and still be a Drakean. Or at least that's one interpretation of what they call the Circle. A business can't let itself be taken over by an organization with all the predictability of a roulette wheel."

"How likely is it that the Union's going to win?"

"That depends." McGaughy's voice was so soft I could barely hear him over the plash of the waterfall. "Here, read this." He pulled a sheaf of photocopy paper from the breast pocket of his shiny suit and held it out diffidently. I scanned a typed legal document, dated several years ago, headed *Last Will and Testament,* signed at the end by Charles Brockden Kilby. Obviously the first of his two wills.

"A model of good sense and sound procedure," McGaughy remarked as I skimmed the will. "You'll notice it was executed here in Jersey but Ms. Nixon-Markson assures me that it complies with the formal requirements of each of the states that claimed Chuck as theirs."

I looked up from the document as its key provisions elbowed their way into what I use for a brain. "By this will," I said, "Kilby leaves half his stock in Omnitron to the corporation itself."

"Right," McGaughy beamed.

"And the other half to you."

"Right," he beamed.

No wonder all the honchos are so deferential to this little imp, I thought.

"But if the California court decides that the second will is his true last will, you and the corporation get nothing?"

"Right." He wasn't beaming any more.

"So tell me about that other will."

McGaughy squinched his eyes shut and began to paint for me a word picture of the last moments in Kilby's life. Keeping in mind that the old trickster hadn't been on the spot but was merely recounting what witnesses had told him or others, he did a fantastically vivid job. A work shift went off duty, and hundreds of Omnitron grunts streamed past the glass walls of the garden and out to distant parking lots, and I hardly noticed. I was up in the clouds with the Lear jet, thirty thousand feet over west central Pennsylvania, with Kilby and the then head of the corporate legal staff, Martin Genetelli, as they conferred on various matters in the plane's plushly appointed lounge. The only other human on board is the pilot up front in the cockpit. Suddenly Kilby turns white, falls back in his upholstered armchair as if he's been pole-axed, fights for breath and claws at his chest and seems to want to rip his jacket and shirt off. For a few seconds Genetelli just sits there bug-eyed with fright. Then he watches Kilby calmly pull a sheet of Omnitron bond stationery out of the drawer of the built-in desk, and take the Cross pen out of his shirt pocket, and turn his back on Genetelli and bend over the desk's surface and, for perhaps fifty to sixty seconds, put words on the page. Then he folds the sheet in thirds, reaches into the desk drawer for an envelope, puts the paper in the envelope, and puts the envelope in his jacket pocket. Then without making a sound he falls over on the plane floor. Somehow Genetelli makes himself move. Knowing no first aid himself, he stumbles out of the lounge and races down the length of the jet to the cockpit and tears open the door and yells for the pilot—who puts the jet on automatic and runs back to the lounge with Genetelli and bends over Kilby and tries to administer CPR. Too late. The pilot goes back to the cockpit and radios the nearest airfield for emergency authorization to land and have an EMS team ready for action. Permission granted. The Lear jet touches down smoothly at a small boondocks strip. The waiting paramedics confirm that Kilby died within a minute or two of when the coronary hit him. There are state cops and airfield officials on the scene. One cop notices a corner of the envelope sticking out of the pocket of Kilby's now discarded jacket. He gives it to the state officer in charge, who reads it, senses it might be damned important, seals it in an evidence envelope, and gives the still shook-up Genetelli a receipt.

"And that was the second will?"

"In all its glorious simplicity," McGaughy said. "We

have a photocopy upstairs for you but I can recite it word for word. First there's the date, just in numerals, 8/11/84. Then the text. 'This is my last will and testament, revoking all previous wills. I leave my entire estate to The Drakean Union, a religious corporation. I appoint Martin Genetelli executor of my estate.' Then his signature."

"He wrote out his full name?"

"Yes. Charles Brockden Kilby."

"And that's a valid will?"

"It is," McGaughy said, "in the nineteen or twenty states that La Verne told me recognize holographic wills at all. Unfortunately two of the states that do, namely Texas and California, are among the seven that have claimed Chuck as their domiciliary."

"So," I said, striving gamely to approach the problem like a lawyer, "if the Supreme Court affirms that Calamannon fellow's decision that California was Kilby's domicile, or if it decides he was domiciled in Texas, then the holographic will counts as his last will and the Drakean Union winds up owning all of his stock in Omnitron."

"Brilliantly phrased." McGaughy murmured.

"But if the Court decides Kilby died domiciled anywhere else—and Professor Donovan doesn't think that's likely—then the holographic will isn't worth the paper it was written on, the earlier will controls, and Kilby's stock in Omnitron is split fifty-fifty between the corporation and you."

"I could almost believe you are a legal eagle yourself," McGaughy said. "You're a *very* quick study, Mr. Tur—Lattman. The status of the case right now is that Chuck's earlier will has been offered for probate in each of the seven states claiming him, and the Drakeans have offered the holographic will for probate in Texas and California. Proceedings in all seven states are on hold until the Supreme Court reviews Calamannon's decision in favor of California."

"Fine," I said. "But I still don't see why you people think you need a private investigator."

"Congratulations!" McGaughy chuckled gleefully over the hiss and rush of the artificial waterfall. "You've penetrated to the innermost layer of our problem. You see, in order to prevail even in California the Drakeans have to establish that the holographic will is in Chuck Kilby's handwriting. And that, I assure you, is easier said than done. Perhaps if you've read anything about Chuck you'll know why?"

Fragments of newsmagazine stories about the brouhaha over the microchip mogul's two wills all of a sudden came back to me. "His handwriting," I said slowly. "Wasn't he allergic to putting stuff down on paper in his own handwriting?"

"Chuck had a very sad childhood," McGaughy said. From his voice and his eyes I sensed that he had withdrawn into a private place inside himself. "Both his parents were alcoholics and fought like a pair of wildcats. He grew up almost totally without love. No surprise that he was a moody and introspective kid. Do you know how he escaped?"

I shook my head no.

"Into books. Into science and technology. He poured all his love into a discipline, something that couldn't love him back and therefore couldn't make him miserable the way his parents had."

"But it could make him very rich," I cut in.

"So it did. Made him into a moody, self-imprisoned young man who couldn't love or trust another human being. He was *afraid* of love. He was afraid of commitment. And from his perspective, signing his name to anything was a form of commitment. Once he became successful, which was very early in his career, he structured both his business life and his personal life so that he would almost never have to put pen to paper. He delegated so much power within the company he made Mr. Reagan look like a hands-on manager by comparison. When he had to communicate he used dictating equipment, typewriters, eventually word processors. He always kept a Cross pen in his shirt pocket but was never seen using it except that once, in the Lear jet, just before he died. You see, he had this paranoid fear that if specimens of his handwriting or signature were easily available, even within Omnitron, he'd be ripped off somehow."

"Didn't you say he wrote poetry?" I asked.

"On the word processor."

"What did he do with the stuff?"

"Gave them to me." McGaughy smiled shyly. "I saved them."

"So maybe," I said, "there was one person he did love and trust."

I expected the little gnome to nod benevolently like a jack-in-the-box and display some quiet pride that he and he alone had gotten through to the strange young genius. I was disappointed. "Chuck and I go back a long way," he replied without emotion. "I think he was as close to me as he could be to anyone. I can't honestly tell you he loved or trusted me. If he'd lived longer . . ."

"A man who can't commit himself to anyone or anything," I said, "makes a superhuman effort in his last seconds of life and writes a holographic will leaving everything to a religion. Doesn't seem in character."

"Ah," McGaughy sighed. "I was waiting for you to make that point. Now perhaps you understand even more why you are needed here."

No perhaps about it. Enlightenment was pouring down on me like the plashing waterfall. "So you think the Drakean Union forged that will and killed your protégé,"

I said, "and you want me to pay them back." I confess that the prospect of conducting a jihad against a murderous religion intoxicated me. No wonder the old cackler needed Milo's gentle touch!

"I'm afraid it's not that simple," McGaughy said, a refrain I had been hearing all too many times this gloomy afternoon. "There is not a shred of medical basis for believing Chuck died of anything but a coronary. All the postmortem documents are upstairs waiting for you."

"But if he was murdered and a forged will planted on his body," I said, "only this Genetelli character could have done it. They were alone on the Lear jet, right?"

"Except for the pilot," McGaughy agreed.

"So the way to begin is by breaking down Genetelli. Who is he? Where did he come from? Who hired him as your house counsel? Does he belong to the Drakean Union? How religious is he? Would he commit a murder to enrich the faith? Does he have any medical background so that he might know of a way to kill someone and make it look like a coronary?" The questions were shooting out of me like bullets from an Uzi.

"His personnel file is also upstairs waiting for you," McGaughy said.

How could he have known that that was just what I was about to ask for? "Your middle initial must stand for Prescient," I said. "Anytime you want a job with the Lattman Agency, it's yours."

The offer provoked out of McGaughy a strange satisfied sound almost like the purring of a cat. "If the Drakean Union winds up controlling this company," he said, "I may just take you up on that." He bowed his head as if in prayer until his plastic-rimmed specs were almost touching the plastic shell of his wristwatch. "About an hour yet till dinner," he said. "Perhaps I should take you back up and put you in an office where you can go through the paperwork."

I scraped my wrought-iron chair back and treated myself to a seventh-inning stretch. "I don't suppose there's any chance Genetelli is invited to this dinner party?"

"Oh, we'd be delighted to have you meet him," McGaughy beamed. "But I'm afraid it can't be done. You see, that's another of the little problems we face. Martin Genetelli disappeared not long after Chuck's death. No one has seen him for well over a year. No one knows if he's alive or dead."

So that's how the opening was created that was now being filled by La Verne De Nise Nixon-Markson! Almost without my knowing it, the data processing neurons I keep in my head were sorting out the possibilities. Genetelli's testimony was obviously going to be crucial to the Drakean Union's chances of success in court. If he was alive, most likely the Union was keeping him underground until he was needed. If he was dead, it might mean anything. It might even mean that someone at Omnitron had had him snuffed so as to shut his mouth. I didn't think McGaughy would do it, and I didn't think Fest or Vanderwell could do it, but I wouldn't have put it past Colonel Shaw.

It was on those mental notes that I followed McGaughy across the greenery of the executive garden and over to the elevator, which whisked us back to the Omnitron building's summit.

4

As to his food, the Master never tired of rice so long as it was clean and pure, nor of hashed meats when finely minced . . . He would not eat anything that was not properly cut or that was not served with its proper sauce.

The Analects of Confucius, X:8

I EARNED MY dinner by reading what is mockingly known as Business English.

Ensconced in a quiet cubbyhole furnished with desk, chair, and not much else, I went over the bulging file stenciled *MEDICAL* in bold red caps. Although I read without expertise and had to skip much of the jargon, I reached the end of the file convinced that Charles Brockden Kilby had died a natural death. Not only had his coronary been prefigured by all sorts of indications from his last few years of physicals, it had been confirmed by a team of the leading forensic pathologists in the United States, who had been retained by Omnitron to autopsy Kilby's body. The top people in their field, knowing who was paying their fees, knowing (I assumed) that Omnitron wanted desperately to discredit that holographic will, knowing that anything not kosher about his death would go a hell of a long step toward that goal, found zilch. I'd be wasting my time if I tried to topple that mountain of medical evidence.

Next I turned to the personnel file on Martin Genetelli,

which struck me as a strangely skimpy pile of paper considering the man's importance to the company. There was a glossy of the head and shoulders photo that appeared in the corporate brochure, and another showing what he looked like from crown to toe: squat, beer-bellied, broad in the beam, the sort of guy whose like could be found in abundance downing boilermakers in every working-class bar in Hoboken. According to the file he was thirty-two years old, Jersey born and bred, a graduate of St. Peter's College in Jersey City and of Marquette University Law School in Milwaukee, where he was an associate editor of the *Law Review*. He had come back to New Jersey, taken and passed the state bar exam, was hired as a staff lawyer in Omnitron's legal department, and was running the department three years later. Single, both parents dead. Listed his religion as Roman Catholic. Lived alone in a small tract house on a quiet little street in Penns Neck, which is a suburb within easy commuting distance of Princeton and Omnitron. The file didn't suggest any close friendship between Genetelli and Charles Kilby that would account for Kilby having named him executor in his holographic will, but then by all reports Kilby hadn't really been close to anybody—except possibly McGaughy, whom he might have ruled out on grounds of age and lack of a law degree—and so his choice of Genetelli might have made sense *faute de mieux*. In any event, after he dropped down the rabbit hole, Omnitron had brought in a discreet but conventional private agency to find him, but they had gotten nowhere, although it took them many billable hours to do so. At this late date I didn't think I could do any better.

Last but far from thinnest of the files was the one stenciled *Young, Constance W.* It was a name that, as far as I could recall, I hadn't heard drop from the lips of any of the Omnitron hangers-on who'd been lecturing at me or dialoguing with me since late morning. But within three minutes of my opening the file, I saw as clearly as I saw my own hand in front of my eyes that the control of this high-tech empire might very well hinge on the lady.

The first item in the file was the letter. Meticulously typed, addressed to Colonel Shaw by his full name and proper corporate title, dated five and a half weeks ago, composed on plain bond paper straight out of a discount store.

5407 Sturges Place
Monckton, Illinois 62005
September 10, 1985

Whitfield J. Shaw, President
Omnitron Technologies, Inc.
Princeton Junction, N.J. 08540

Dear Colonel Shaw:

I have been following with interest the regrettably brief and sketchy accounts in the media on the dispute over the estate of the late Charles Brockden Kilby, founder of Omnitron. It is my understanding that the parties to the dispute are desperately in need of specimens of Mr. Kilby's handwriting in order to prove or disprove the authenticity of the holographic will he is alleged to have made out just before his death.

Charles Kilby and I were students together at Monckton High School during the middle and late 1960s. I happen to have thirty-two (32) substantial specimens of Charles's handwriting in the form of poems he wrote to me during that period. Enclosed you will find a photocopy of one such poem. Please forgive the slightly blurred reproduction.

For the sum of two million dollars ($2,000,000.00), payable half in advance and half on completion of my part of the proposed contract, I will sell Omnitron the manuscripts of the thirty-two poems, and I will testify under oath as to their authenticity, and as to the circumstances in which they were given to me, at any judicial proceeding where my testimony may be helpful.

As of this writing I am making this offer only to Omnitron. I hope to hear from you at your convenience.

Sincerely,

Constance W. Young

Either the lady was a lawyer or she'd had a legal eagle draft the letter. It was a lovely specimen of high pressure exerted with subtlety. There was no way Shaw could have read it and not said to himself: *My God, how long before she makes the same offer to the Drakean Union?* Any suspicion that he might be the target of a scam would come later, if at all.

Attached to the letter by a staple was a poor but legible photocopy of what I would charitably describe as a piece of verse. Sixteen lines, four quatrains, handwritten, hot from the youthful heart:

My dear, no mouse will ever chew
Our sacred cheese of love
Nor will I e'er see buzzard wings
Upon my turtledove.

Out of respect for the reader's sensibilities I shall resist the urge to quote the rest of this epic. I am no poetry critic nor even a devotee, but if the Omnitron job was going to entail my reading the other thirty-one specimens of Kilby's adolescent love mush, I knew I'd be earning my fee.

The rest of the file filled me in on the steps Shaw had taken since the letter's arrival. There was a memorandum from La Verne De Nise Nixon-Markson on whether it was legal for Constance Young to sell her testimony. There was a report from an examiner of questioned documents, who was fussily noncommittal about whether the photocopied poem came from the same hand that had penned the holographic will but expressing the view that the verse might well be authentic. There was a hefty sheaf of paperwork from a PI outfit in Chicago that Shaw had retained to check the lady out. From all that they could discover in a couple of weeks, she was the genuine article. They had glommed Monckton High student records showing that a Constance Williams had been enrolled there at the same time as Kilby. According to those records, both had graduated in 1967, Kilby with high honors in science. They had discreetly interviewed three other members of that year's crop of Monckies, who recollected that Kilby had indeed been infatuated for a time with the Williams chick, although the consensus of the trio was that she had preferred the captain of the school's legendary football eleven, the Monckton Wombats. The Windy City's answer to Philip Marlowe had snapped undetected a roll of photographs of the woman calling herself Constance W. Young and living at 5407 Sturges Place: slender, sleek-bodied, fine-boned, dark straight hair framing features of a startling intensity. Not at all a shabby lady. The eyes had found a 1971 Iowa marriage license between Constance Williams and a Jonathan B. Young, and clippings from a newspaper published in Lamoni, Iowa and dated 1976, reporting that Jonathan B. Young, a local real estate broker, had died of cancer, survived by his widow, the former Constance

Williams, and no children. Copies of all these documents were in the file. Likewise a copy of the lease Constance W. Young had signed for the house on Sturges Place. Then came the reports of two peepers who had shadowed the lady for a week. If Spade and Spenser were to be trusted, she was leading a dull life. No job. No safe deposit box at the bank she patronized nor apparently anywhere else in Monckton either. No close friends or regular visitors. No socializing to speak of. The report speculated that the pain of losing her husband might not yet have worn away. Her house was equipped with an electronic alarm system connected to all the doors and windows so that she was all but invulnerable to the garden variety of burglar. The gadgetry hadn't come with the house. She'd had the system installed at her own expense right after moving in.

"She expects to be visited," I said to myself, or at least I thought it was to myself. Maybe I'd spoken aloud. Maybe McGaughy had heard me thinking. Already there was little I would put beyond the powers of that uncanny elf. In any event, at the precise moment that thought entered my brain and the words (if any) exited my mouth, the door to the cubbyhole clicked open and McGaughy stood facing me in the aperture.

"I trust you won't disappoint her," he said. "Ready for dinner? By the way, please overlook Herb Vanderwell's affliction. It only bothers him outside of business meetings."

The Omnitron executive dining room and kitchen on the west side of the top floor was a beauty, with the decor of a five-star restaurant enfolded in a high-tech business hive. The antique satin floor-to-ceiling drapes were pulled back and likewise the overhead roof panels, exposing the loveliness of the at long last fog-free evening. The play of moonlight, highway lights, and distant house and office lights was dazzling. No wonder Kilby had felt the need to versify on the subject. The symphony of light dwarfed the dining room's furnishings, which were stunning enough in their own right: half a dozen huge burnished ovals of Honduras mahogany, discreet Sarouks dotting the parquet, inlaid china cupboards lit from within to display Steuben glass and Imari bowls and Wedgwood. Only one of the six tables was set up for service. I didn't think it was happenstance that no other Omnitron poohbahs were entertaining tonight. My place at the oval was between McGaughy and Landy and more or less across from Colonel Shaw, who was flanked by toadpuss Fest and nerdmouth Vanderwell. Between Landy and Fest sat Ms. Nixon-Markson, plucking nervously at her pale gray linen napkin like a stranger in a strange land. I settled into my diamond-tufted armchair and scanned the delicately printed menu card propped on my plate, and waited for the veterans of this mess hall to order and give me a cue. A Vietnamese in a white bolero jacket came to the table and stood there patiently awaiting our pleasure, while a pair of Hispanic ladies commuted between the swing door to the kitchen and a satinwood-inlayed brandy board against one wall, bringing out with each circuit a cluster of silver chafing dishes from which exotic aromas dribbled forth.

"We're lucky tonight," Shaw rumbled from across the oval. He was nursing a goblet that held Lillet vermouth on the rocks with a twist of orange. "If you're on a diet, Mr. Lattman, prepare to break it now." His underlings chuckled diplomatically at the line. McGaughy simply smacked his lips. "For security reasons we'll serve ourselves," the colonel added, and got to his feet and went over to the brandy board to inspect the viands. The chafing dishes were aligned on the gleaming mahogany as neat as a Marine platoon on the parade ground: pâtés, caviar, ravioli stuffed with escargot, fresh salmon in a ginger sauce, brioche of escargot and Roquefort cheese, scallop mousse, and duckling consommé. I helped myself to a little of each as auto lights in the distance made diamond and ruby magic on the window wall. The rest of the evening's dialogue was punctuated by one of the finest meals of my life. The inadequacy of words compels me to just hit the high spots.

"I-I t-take it then that you h-h-had time to g-go through the f-f-files, Mr. Latt-Lattman?" That was Vanderwell, his affliction in full regalia now that he wasn't in a business environment. He had passed up the temptations on the sideboard and ordered a red fig sherbet from the menu, the better to talk while eating.

"Most of them," I said. I took another sip of the wine, a fine fruity Chardonnay from Guenoc. "Everything does seem to hang on this Mrs. Young and the poem about the mouse."

"If you can call that a poem," hazarded Fest from inside a mouthful of snailed ravioli.

"Some mouse," grunted Dave Landy between spoonfuls of the consommé. "That mouse be worth ninety million dollars a year to someone." He kept darting glances to his left at La Verne Nixon-Markson as if looking for approval. She smiled at him coolly.

"Let me get something straight," I said. "I'm not a lawyer and Professor Donovan didn't discuss the point this afternoon, but it's my understanding that in a will contest, if there's any doubt about the authenticity of a will that's offered for probate, it's up to the person offering the will to prove it's authentic. Right?"

"The risk of nonpersuasion is on the proponent," said our law lady, which meant, I think, that she agreed with me.

"And as things stand now," I went on, "unless Mrs. Young offers her poems and testimony to the Drakean

Union, they don't stand much of a chance of proving the handwriting on that holographic will is Mr. Kilby's."

"Probably not," the colonel said cautiously, sighting at me along the stem of his unlit pipe. "What's the point?"

"Yet according to her letter," I continued, "she's offering the stuff to you first, not to them. Right?" General nodding in the affirmative. "And once you're convinced the lady and the poems are the real thing, it's very much in your interest to cut a deal with her. Shred the poems, bury the lady where the Union can't find her—that's a figure of speech of course—and watch them quietly go bananas trying to find other specimens of Kilby's handwriting."

My bald-faced précis of where the company's interests lay was apparently a bit too raw for Vice-President Fest, who spluttered into his caviar and turned red as a lox and coughed and cleared his pipes with a long swallow of ice water. "Now just one darn minute," he protested nobly. "Assuming Mr. Kilby gave the woman those pieces of paper, they belong to her. They're her property. She can sell them to whoever she wants for whatever she can get. And whoever buys them can do what they please with them. Isn't that right?" He turned to Ms. Nixon-Markson, who agreed that he was correct. "And that includes throwing them into the trash where they belong. Just because they're covered with so-called poetry doesn't require us or the Young woman or anyone else to preserve them."

"Well, except that . . ." And Ms. Nixon-Markson launched into an impromptu but obviously preresearched monologue on the law of intellectual property and the rights of owners of unpublished manuscripts as opposed to the rights of the estate of the author. The discourse couldn't have been timed more perfectly. It allowed Colonel Shaw to press a concealed buzzer that summoned the kitchen help to clear away the appetizers and bring on the main courses and not hear a damn thing but lawyer talk while they were doing it. I wasn't listening to the legal jargon, and I wasn't paying attention to the bus persons. I was watching the faces of my fellow diners. Shaw and Fest and Vanderwell looked bored. McGaughy looked bemused. Landy looked entranced. By the time the lecture on copyright was behind us, a wondrous assortment of entrees was in front of us. Fest attacked his beef tournedos in three-mustard sauce without waiting for his commanding officer to begin. He had been vindicated. He wasn't involved in anything that was illegal, no indeed.

"And it's the s-same th-thing when it comes to her t-testi-testimony," offered Vice-President Vanderwell, gazing fondly through his bifocals at the mushroom-topped medallions of veal before him. "She's not offering to c-commit p-perjury, is she?"

"Of course not," chimed in McGaughy, who had chosen a simple repast of lightly grilled brill and cherry tomatoes stuffed with finely diced jalapeño peppers. Remembering our mobile luncheon, I wondered if the little gnome ever ate meat. "All she says is that if the company pays her two million dollars she'll give us the poems plus her truthful testimony. Let the chips fall where they may." He turned on me with an almost wounded look in his pale old eyes as if I had betrayed him. "Surely you're not afraid of the legal complications, Mr. Lattman?" he said, meaning something known only to him and his cohort Landy, and of course to me.

It was time to change the subject. I busied myself with duckling and sweet garlic sauce and a 1977 Sterling reserve cabernet sauvignon. Before I had figured out what to say next, Colonel Shaw took the conversational ball into his own court.

"What we do if we decide Mrs. Young and the poems

are genuine," he said, "is up to us. What we do if we decide they're fakes is another matter. In that case our course is clear. We don't pay her a cent, and we don't give a damn whether she cuts a deal with the Drakean Union. No, as you were, as you were. We light candles and pray she does cut a deal with them, because then when she goes on the witness stand for them we can rip her in shreds with the proof that she's pulled a scam."

"Do you understand your assignment now?" McGaughy half-whispered in my ear. "You're to make that judgment call for us. A judgment," he added slyly, "that no one is better qualified to make than you." On the principle, no doubt, that one should set a confidence person to catch a confidence person.

"And I'm also to find Martin Genetelli if I can," I said. "Because if he's alive and the Drakeans are keeping him under wraps until these probate hearings, and if he testifies that he saw Kilby write that holographic will, the Drakeans may win the contest even without the mouse poems."

"Oh, definitely," the colonel echoed. "Find Marty if you can."

"And what do I do with him if I do find him?"

"You let us know," the colonel said softly.

And it went without saying that everyone sitting around that lavishly accoutered table knew as well as they knew their own names and the details of their own compensation packages that there was no way I could make that judgment call on the authenticity of the poems without getting hold of them, and that Mrs. Young was hardly likely to hand over the poems to me or anyone else until the cash was in her hands, which meant that these boardroom mandarins were de facto engaging me to visit the lady unannounced and steal the stuff, at least temporarily. But of course they weren't engaging me to do anything illegal and neither they individually nor

Omnitron as an institution would be responsible if I should prove overenthusiastic and slip my leash and violate a law or three. But on all these matters the room maintained a dignified and impenetrable silence. Such is the way business is done in America.

"And my fee for making all these judgments," I said, "is one million dollars, plus expenses. Half in advance, cash or certified check."

"Agreed," Shaw said without a microsecond's hesitation. The others around the table grunted and nodded affirmance as if they really had a say in the matter. Even Landy let out with a murmured: "Right on."

"But," the colonel said, "we have one condition. A couple of our own people will also go to Monckton, to protect our interests."

I looked up from the remnants of my bird in mild shock. "If you're paying me a million dollars to do this job, don't you think I can find helpers of my own if I need them?"

"Spend two minutes with a map of western Illinois," Shaw said, "and you'll know you're going to need them."

Before I could ask what that crack was supposed to mean, dear old McGaughy chimed in. "You'll never find help like Dave and me," he cackled merrily. "We're the ones that are going."

In light of what those two knew about me and the others didn't, I judged it prudent to stifle protest and finish my wine. Shaw touched the buzzer and the kitchen help rematerialized and whisked away the dishes and wineglasses and brought out the dessert, which was a millefeuille, a cake of many layers, each one being of a different flavor and variety of chocolate, from velvet black to milk-light, and a magnificent chocolate mousse down the middle. It was served with the Mysore coffee I drink at home—coincidence, or again the McGaughy touch?—and with a buffet of liqueurs, drambuie and amaretto and creme de menthe and triple sec and Grand Marnier and an Israeli import called Sabra that brought back memories of a woman I'd never see again. We settled the money details over cordials and I shook hands all around, and Landy ran off to fetch me the files, and McGaughy escorted me to the silver-gray stretch limo. With Landy again behind the wheel and McGaughy again in the opposite corner of the velour-upholstered rear compartment we glided as if on silken springs through the night silences of New Jersey and through the Tunnel and back to midtown Manhattan and my George Boyd condo on the rim of Central Park. "Here," McGaughy said as I was about to exit the limo, and handed me one more thing to carry in with me, an unmarked manila envelope. "Something for you to study in the morning. I'll call you." The limo slipped away into the eastbound traffic stream, and I gave a friendly nod to the doorman and passed through the small mirrored lobby to the elevator and up to the door of my own roost, which I keyed open, true to McGaughy's word, at exactly three minutes to midnight.

That damned little sorcerer. How had he known me?

5

Mencius said: Learn widely and go into what you have learned in detail, so that in the end you can return to the essential.

Mencius, IV B: 15

LETTER BOMB.

At a few minutes past eight the next morning, when I was shaved, showered, and most of the way through toweling myself, that marrow-freezing little phrase leapt into my head. I have no idea what put it there. Maybe there had been a news item about the IRA on my bathroom radio while I'd been scraping the face, and I subconsciously connected the story with the Irish sound of the name McGaughy. However it happened, the result was a split-second anxiety attack, a sudden obsessive certainty that the tan manila envelope the old ferret had handed me last night was rigged to explode in my eyes when I slit it open.

It was only after I was half dressed and half goofy with worry that the voice of sense spoke to me. For what earthly reason would McGaughy want me dead or maimed when it was he who had nudged me into the Omnitron mess, he who had conjured out of the corporation treasury an advance for me of half a million dollars, he who had kept two of my major cover identities intact when he could have blown them with a word?

I brewed a pot of Mysore, poured a glass of grapefruit juice, popped croissants into the microwave, and occupied myself over breakfast with trying to answer my own question and got nowhere.

All life is risk. Over my second cup of coffee I took my letter opener and tore into the manila envelope. Gently.

Nothing happened.

I shook out the envelope's contents onto the dining table and spread the papers across the mahogany in organized piles. The heftiest item was a paperbound book of about the dimensions of a small city's phone directory. Blue-gray letters against a royal purple background read: *Barnabas Drake University, General Bulletin, 1985–1986*. The lower two-thirds of the cover was filled by a design in the same colors, one which I had seen hundreds of times before but had never paid attention to till now. A simple blue-gray oval. The egg. What Drakeans insisted on calling the Circle. The sign of the Union, as familiar as the cross or the crescent or the hammer and sickle. A royal purple band cutting through the center of the egg bore the initials BDU.

I spent half an hour flipping through the catalogue. It taught me that the president of Barnabas Drake University was Dr. Joseph Rathjen, the same silver-thatched hypnotic-voiced matinee idol who for the past quarter century had been the high ferio—what in Catholicism would be called the pope or in Islam the ayatollah—of the Drakean Union. His official photograph in the catalogue was flanked by aerial shots of the BDU campus, its majestic buildings nestled on the edge of the high bluffs overlooking the Illinois River. I learned of the cornucopia of intellectual and cultural opportunities offered by dear old BDU, of the rich resources of its library, the world-renowned scholarly achievements of its faculty, the mighty tomes coughed out by the university press, the stunning array of Barnabas Drake manuscripts and memorabilia that were preserved in a special subterranean vault equipped with a carbon dioxide fire protection system that, once its sensors detected heat, would flood the chamber with gas within thirty to sixty seconds and leave the flame not an atom of oxygen to feed on. I learned that attendance at BDU was restricted to highly committed Drakeans who scored in the top twenty percentile on the Scholastic Aptitude Test and also aced an exam on the history and dogma of the Union that the university gave to all who applied for admission. Tuition was astronomical.

Next I turned to the second heftiest item from the manila envelope, a crisp new auto club map headed *Western Illinois and Eastern Missouri.* I spread the map across the table and smoothed out its creases and eyeballed the urban patch on the east bank of the Mississippi that was labeled *Monckton.* On paper at least it looked like a thriving metrop, smack along Illinois's Great River Road, forty or fifty miles north of St. Louis. The city was crisscrossed by three interstate highways, enjoyed its own international airport, and lay within easy driving distance of three state parks.

And also within easy driving distance of something else. About thirty miles west of Monckton along the Great River Road, just below the point where the Illinois River merges with the Mississippi, the map showed a grayish patch that in letters barely visible to the naked eye was marked *Barnabas Drake University.*

I began to see why McGaughy had stuck the map in my war bag.

Then I saw something else on the map, but I was prepared for this one. Just a few dozen miles west of BDU, a long and vaguely snake-shaped tongue of land between the Illinois and the Mississippi Rivers was lettered *Union Island.* Click! The city of Monckton, the campus of Barnabas Drake University, and the world headquarters of the Drakean Union were within two hours' drive from one another. I had seen bigger coincidences in my life, but another of those voices in my head told me that this wasn't one of them.

Now I remembered that crack Colonel Shaw had made during our Lucullan feast last night, something to the effect that if I'd spend two minutes with a map of the area I'd see why I was going to need help. And a true prophet he turned out to be. Visiting Monckton on a job that threatened the economic interests of the Drakean Union would be very much like visiting the zoo and sticking my head in the lion's mouth. I began to think seriously about giving back my retainer to Omnitron and walking away from this one.

During which cogitation my phone rang. Mechanically I snatched up the handset and said "George Boyd" into the mouthpiece.

"What, no good morning?" That dry cackle could belong to no one in the world but McGaughy. "Have you studied the map yet?"

"Just caught all the connections a few minutes ago," I said. "What do—"

"And what do you make of them?"

"I was just asking you the same question. You claim you knew Chuck Kilby better than anyone else. He grew up in a city that I suspect must be pretty well saturated with Drakean influence, the way Salt Lake City is by the Mormons. Did he ever talk to you about being exposed to Drakeanism as a kid? Were his parents Drakeans? How about the teachers at Monckton High that he admired, if any?"

There was an uncharacteristic silence on the far end of the wire. I could picture McGaughy standing at his phone, ransacking his memories of what Kilby had told him about his youth. "I . . . just can't answer that with any assurance," he said at last. "There was so much buried inside him that, even with me, he couldn't or wouldn't let out. If he'd lived a few years longer . . . Anyway, I just don't know. If you're right, I suppose it might account for his holographic will. Is that what you're thinking?"

"It's certainly what the Union will argue," I said. "It would make the second will a hell of a lot more credible if that sort of connection between Kilby and Drakeanism could be established."

"And make it so much less credible if no one could make the connection?"

"Maybe," I said. "Ask Professor Donovan, that's his department."

"Do you think it's worth following up?"

"Not to me, my plate's full as it is. You might want to talk it over with Donovan and Shaw. If you want to pursue it, you could always have that Chicago PI outfit send a team back to Monckton to hunt for Drakean connections in Kilby's past. I'm not sure it matters much one way or the other. Suppose the Union could find a Drakean in Monckton who was sort of a father figure to Kilby in his formative years. They'd still have to prove the authenticity of the handwriting on that will. Everything stands or falls on the handwriting."

"Then you'll be going to Monckton soon to investigate that aspect of the case?"

"Not soon," I said. "Eventually."

"When?" he pressed me.

I discovered to my amazement that my qualms of a few minutes before had vanished. Willy nilly or nilly willy, I was in this mess all the way. "Maybe in two weeks. Which reminds me. Just for security's sake, please don't call me here again. If I need anything I'll call you at Omnitron."

"Fine," he said. "Better yet, call Dave Landy. I'm sending him to New York this morning. The Essex

House Hotel is just a short walk from your place. I'll have him stay there, just in case you need a shadow or a bodyguard or general assistant on short notice. Let him know when you leave for Monckton, and he'll join you a day or two later. I'll be around too if you need me."

"I wish the two of you would stay home," I said.

"You only think you wish we'd stay home," he said.

A moment later the line was dead, and I was alone again with my premonitions.

I folded the map of western Illinois back into its original shape and put it aside with the BDU catalogue and took a quick look at the rest of what had been in the manila envelope. Most of it was promotional brochures, each one headed with the word *Monckton* in large caps. I decided to save those for later.

Last but far from least was a sheaf of typed pages that looked like the bibliography from a student's term paper, but without the body of the paper. Titles of books in English, books in German, scholarly articles in theological journals in at least five languages, were arranged neatly in alphabetical order. In one way or another they all seemed to be about the life or religious thought of Barnabas Drake. Attached to the pages with a staple was a three-by-five notecard with a brief handwritten message: "This might help in your work. McG."

There was no way he could have put this package together after our gunpoint meeting yesterday around noon, so he must have had it ready before then, knowing, or guessing, or gambling, that my answer to Omnitron's offer would be a Yes. That uncanny old weasel was beginning to grate on my nerves. But not enough to tempt me to bow out again.

That afternoon I packed a bag, took the elevator to the lobby, slipped out of the condo while the doorman's back was turned, and blended into the stream of pedestrians eastbound on Fifty-ninth Street. It was a brisk fall day with clouds of all shades of gray scudding across the sky but no threat of rain. At Lexington I pointed myself south and at the corner of Fiftieth I turned in, presented myself at the registration desk of the Hotel Beverly, and claimed the suite I'd reserved earlier in the day under one of the several identities I keep in my bureau drawer for just such occasions as this. Unpacked, I went out again and resumed my nice little walk, my destination this time being the lion-guarded portals of the main branch of the New York Public Library. My daytime home for the next week.

With my self-imposed deadline for migrating to Monckton a scant fourteen days in the future, there was no way even a quick study such as I modestly claim to be could absorb everything listed in McGaughy's bibliography. I had to content myself with a random sample. My first stop was a couple of survey articles on the Drakean Union from the back numbers of *The New Yorker* and *Business Week*. These pieces gave me an overview of the terrain just as McGaughy's map had, except that with the articles you had to read between the lines. I learned a lot.

I learned about the obsession in Barnabas Drake's writings with the concept of the Circle and the obsession in the Drakean artwork and architecture, including the stuff created in his lifetime, with the shape of the egg. Either Barnabas had made no distinction between the forms or he needed glasses. I learned about the traditional Drakean breakfast, how he had commanded all believers to start off each morning as he had himself, with an apple, an orange, and a hard-boiled egg, and how that combo was now offered on the menus of two-thirds of the major hotel and restaurant chains in America. I discovered that Barnabas's complete works ran to seventy-two thick volumes, published in a deluxe edition by Barnabas Drake University Press, and that every Drakean was required to buy at least a book a year from the set. I discovered that the strange titles bestowed upon the Drakean hierarchy—ferio and colinory and azana and orent and three or four dozen others of the same ilk—came from the sheet of notepaper found clenched in Barnabas's fist when he'd been found dead. Nonsense syllables to an infidel, inspired wisdom to the believer. I learned about the way Drake's followers in the 1920s had taken over the narrow tongue of farmland peninsula in Calhoun County, Illinois, between the Mississippi and Illinois rivers, and turned it into an island and their own version of the Vatican. I learned that every Drakean family was obliged to spend at least a week a year at one of the regional or national Drakean Circle Camps unless excused by the local orent. With all the financial duties the religion imposed on members, I wasn't surprised to read that its annual income from all sources was estimated in the billions.

On the Union's dealings with the outside world the media tended to report with kid gloves. I found out that the rulers of the Circle didn't mind objective factual accounts of Drakean beliefs and practices and history but took not at all kindly to what they considered negative stereotypes. That the Union kept several powerhouse law firms on annual seven-figure retainers for the sole purpose of bringing huge defamation suits against anyone with the temerity to publish material unfairly critical of the Circle. That any such publication and all its advertisers were likely to be branded as enemies of the Circle in the monthly magazine, *The Drakean,* to which all the faithful were required to subscribe, and that once branded they'd be boycotted across the country. That on the rare occasion when the feds or a state started to look into some aspect of the Union's activities, the hierarchy would unleash its pet civil liberties advocates and fight off the assault with loud squeals about the First Amendment and religious freedom. None of this was ever stated boldly on the page, but if you read carefully and skeptically, the truth bled through the cool and neutral reportage.

When the library closed its doors, I walked back to the Beverly convinced that any true believer in the Circle, given the chance to kill a man and forge a will and thereby enrich the faith by ninety million dollars a year, would have jumped at the chance like an Olympic pole-vaulter. Too bad the forensic pathologists had said Kilby died of a heart attack. Too bad Martin Genetelli had been (at least on paper) a Catholic. The holographic will still looked like the only weak link in the chain.

I spent that evening and the next several evenings in my suite at the Beverly, my ear glued to the phone, making call after call to people in certain service industries that are not listed in the Yellow Pages, ordering equipment I was going to need in the heartland city of Monckton. I spent the next day and most of the following days back at the library, buried in books: a biography of Barnabas Drake, a study of his multitudinous verbal excretions, a history of the Union since his death, a biography of his current successor, the suave and impossibly handsome Dr. Rathjen. I made it a point not to stick to the material McGaughy had recommended but did some half-assed browsing in other books and articles cited in one reference work or another. None of it changed my view of the Union, but then I was born without a religious bone in my body.

Seven solid days of reading that stuff made me want never to crack a book again. I decided to broaden my horizons, try to pick up more information about the Union from a human being.

In my life as George Boyd, cultivated man of Manhattan, I have been invited to scores of genteel receptions, swigged cocktails and noshed munchies with a small army of people at the middle to upper-middle levels of the publishing, academic, and art worlds. A certain number of them must be Drakeans, but since their religion was no more a proper subject of chitchat for them than it is for Christians or Jews, I couldn't identify a single one of my social acquaintances that I could pump on that basis, and from what I'd read it would be the height of dumbness to go that route even if such a person and I had been the best of buddies. But something nagged and gnawed at me, a vague memory of a casual conversation, maybe two-and-a-half or three eyars ago, a converstion in which, at least for a few minutes, the subject had been the Drakean Union. *Remember, damn you!*

It took me most of the day before I did.

Clouds the color of soot were dropping a fine Scottish mist on the city when I turned into the Time-Life Building late that afternoon. I checked the directory and her name wasn't listed, and I checked the receptionist and found out why. She hadn't worked there for two years. I went out again into the drizzle and the tide of pedestrians and on my fifth try found a street phone that worked. I dialed Directory Assistance. Waste of time. Her number was unpublished. I probed deeper into layers of memory.

It had been a cocktail party, perhaps two years ago, somewhere in the Village. Mostly journalism types. The woman had been trying to light a cigarette with a lighter that wouldn't open, and the dry Virginia Slim had slipped from between her lips and landed on my shoe, and the next second her lighter had slipped through her fingers and landed on my other shoe. Three minutes later we were laughing and talking as if we'd known each other for ages. Her name was Sarah Rogers. She was taller than I and had taffy-colored hair, high cheekbones, an anorexic figure, and tension lines around her dark brown eyes. She might have been a model or an actress but she said she was the chief assistant to the religion editor of *Time*. She was thirty-two, divorced, and raising a four-year-old daughter. Now that my memory was in high gear I remembered any number of casual things she'd told me, but only one of them mattered to me now. I had walked her home after the party—it had been a foggy evening and muggers had been prowling her neighborhood, which was also in the Village, and the escort service had been her idea not mine—and on that walk she had mentioned that she'd just begun research on a major piece for *Time* about the Drakean Union, a piece that with luck might turn into a cover story. From my own research over the past week I knew that *Time* had never run such a story. The project could have been scrubbed for any number of reasons. Thousands of projects are, year in and year out, in the business world, in journalism, in Hollywood. But from the moment I remembered that post-midnight stroll with Sarah Rogers, one of my little voices had been yammering at me to find out why this one had not run.

The only way to begin was to head for the Village, try to locate the apartment building I'd walked her back to that night in the fog, and hope she still lived there. As far as I could recall, it had been a high-rise on West Twelfth Street, almost directly across the street from The New School. I stood at the curb for ten minutes and tried to wave down a cab and didn't get a cab but got my trousers slopped on by a small army of them, roaring through the street puddles. In the end I walked. Blat of horns, squeal of brakes, rumble of subways underfoot, drip of drizzle down my neck, all the way south to Sixth Avenue and Twelfth, where I swung east and slowed to a near crawl, trying to remember what that high-rise had looked like.

And, by God, there it was, smack across from The New School. No one had moved the building. A mean-eyed Hispanic doorman graciously allowed me to buzz her apartment—yes, she still lived there, thanks be—and, when the buzz produced no answer, magnanimously permitted me to give him a note for her, asking her to call me at my Beverly number no matter how late she came in. I trudged back to the corner of Sixth and this time played in luck. A cab actually stopped for me.

It was after six and I was nursing my second bourbon and squinting through the balcony windows at the cacophony of the rush-hour city when the phone rang, and I jumped for it. No one else had the number. It had to be Sarah Rogers. And it was.

". . . Yes, I know it's been a couple of years, but I can still remember walking you home from the party that night as if it were yesterday. How are you doing? Still with *Time?* . . . Oh, free-lancing now . . . And your daughter, what is she now, six, seven? . . . Well, I'll tell you why I wanted you to call. It's been a rotten day and looks like a miserable evening, and I sort of perversely hoped you'd had it a bit rough too today, and I thought I could raise both of our spirits by taking you to dinner, if you're free."

She asked me to hang on a minute and was back on the line in three. "I guess it's okay," she said just a tad dubiously. "My brother's up from Florida on a visit and staying with me, and he said with the weather so yukky he didn't mind at all hanging around here and watching videos with Cathy. So-o-o," she drew out the vowel sound with a nervous giggle, "I guess it's a date!"

One might suppose the stage was set for the sort of dinner scene encountered so often in trashy bestsellers. An eatery momentarily favored by the power people, sumptuous decor, celebrity name-dropping, conspicuous consumption, glitz. One would be dead wrong. Two hours after our phone call, Sarah Rogers and I were sitting across from each other at a simple butcher-block table, amid the low roar of two-hundred-odd diners indistinguishable from ourselves, with a bottle of wine and cheeseburgers en casserole and salads and a basket of sourdough bread in front of us, and beside us a picture window looking out on the varicolored mist-filmed lights of West Fifty-Fifth Street. In terms of value for money, La Fondue may be the best restaurant in New York. Any month in which I can't drop in at least once and order Le Cheeseburger, which is a gigantic burger cooked and served in a casserole of cheese fondue, is a culinary waste. Sarah had never heard of the place, but two minutes after the casseroles were set in front of us she was raving about it.

From her looks she could have used more than one decent meal. She was still pencil-lean, still smoked up a storm, still had the tension lines at her eyes and the keyed-up mannerisms of a raw recruit in a combat zone. But she did seem to be enjoying herself this one evening. After the second glass of burgundy she even smiled a little. I decided to spare her the questions I needed to ask until the last possible moment, then bought her more time by suggesting we share a wedge of La Fondue's icebox cake and top it with coffee and an after-dinner drink. It was only over the coffee that I began to hunt for an opening.

"I can't believe it," she said. "Eating this well and this cheap in midtown. I ought to do a piece on the place."

"I've seen your by-line now and then," I lied. "I guess free-lancing has paid off for you."

"I survive," she said.

"Do you miss *Time?*"

"Now and then. The money was better there, but nowadays I get to spend a lot more time with Cathy, and I do love and adore that little monkey."

"Remember," I said, "that night I walked you home

from the party? You told me you were just beginning a major piece about—oh, hell, what's the name of that religion?—yeah, that's it, the Drakean Union. I subscribe to *Time* and I never saw that article in print. What ever happened—"

That was as far as my question got asked. Her face had gone fishbelly gray under her makeup, and her eyes had taken on the look in the eyes of the deer just before the wolf disembowels it. Her lips trembled. She reached for her brandy snifter and missed it by half a foot, and her groping fingers knocked the glass to the floor, where it splintered with a merry tinkling sound. I held out my own snifter in both hands and tilted it to her lips, and she drained the brandy and coughed and gulped while a busboy came up with dustpan and brush and squatted at our feet and cleared away the mess. The disturbance didn't make a dent in the din that surrounded us, and if a few of the other patrons of La Fondue paused for a moment to glance in our direction, they quickly returned to their own cuisine and conversations. Glasses break every day in every restaurant in New York. A look of terror enters a woman's eyes, and everyone around her minds their own business.

I paid the check and took her out of there as fast as I could without attracting any more attention. Out into the dripping night. Into a cab, a moving shelter where I could hold her hand and try to calm her. I told the hacker to take us east and then just drive around where the traffic was light. The hacker was a woolly-headed old black man whose eyes in the rearview mirror told me that in his time he'd seen sights a hell of a lot stranger than the two of us. He cruised along First and Second Avenues, past storefronts and co-op facades and the neon of singles bars glistening in the mist, until I thought Sarah was halfway normal again and told the guy softly to take us to the Beverly.

Where, thirty minutes later, we sat on the long couch in my suite, with two glasses and the bourbon bottle on the coffee table in front of us, and all the lights off except one floor lamp at the couch's far end. But it wasn't Sarah who was telling me her story, it was I who was telling her mine. A small part of mine anyway. A part that at least two too many people knew already, which paradoxically had emboldened me to take a chance and make it three. Whatever had happened to her, whatever had aborted her piece on the Union and her career at *Time*, and left her quivering whenever she remembered, she'd never open up about it to a cocktail-party pal like George Boyd. She might, however, tell the tale to a certain crusading investigator named Arthur Lattman.

I had no other options so I told her, with my credentials as Lattman and my PI license out on the table for her inspection, that Boyd and Lattman slept every night in the same body. It was a revelation she found hard to swallow.

"You? Lattman?"

"Me Lattman," I said lamely.

"The same Lattman that broke up the murder-for-hire ring in St. Louis a few years ago and put their chief hit man in a wheelchair for life? *Time* ran half a column on that case."

"Something like that," I said, and for another split second, as during the liqueurs at Omnitron's gourmet feast, I was assailed by the memory of a woman I'd never see again, the only woman who had ever truly known me.

"And you've been . . . carrying on this double life as George Boyd for years?"

She seemed aghast at the notion that I could sustain two identities, and my imp of the perverse taunted me to tell her of all the others, but I stoutly resisted. "It's useful," I said simply. "Look at what I tried to do tonight and you'll see how useful. Sarah, I can't tell you the whole story, but I'm investigating the Drakean Union. If it works out, I think I can hurt them bad." I made what struck me as not too wild a leap. "Maybe worse than they hurt you," I said.

She puffed nervously on her cigarette and put it down and took a swallow of bourbon and kept the glass in her hands.

"You know something about my track record," I said. "You know I'm in your corner."

She nodded mechanically, like a puppet.

"Will you tell me what they did to you?"

She stopped nodding and sat there on the couch dead still, not looking at me, not looking at anything. Between the gentle cone of light from the floor lamp and the nightglow through the curtained windows there was nothing but darkness.

"Yes," she said.

It was a long story. In the middle of it she got off the couch abruptly, went over to the phone, and called her apartment to let her brother know that everything was fine and she'd be home a little late and to tuck Cathy in and kiss her goodnight. Her brother probably thought we were in bed. How could he have guessed that we were only talking, or that our talk was forging a relationship between us more intense than sex between strangers?

She had been working on the Union story for five weeks, interviewing people who had never talked to a journalist before, former Drakeans who had left the Circle, children raised by Drakean parents, young lawyers who had handled Drakean business for the firms on retainer to the Union but had been let go when they failed to make partner. All sorts of people, reluctantly and in anguish but also with a certain sense of relief telling all sorts of bizarre anecdotes about what went on within the

Circle. Not for attribution. Never for attribution. Sarah had been accumulating and organizing the material, trying to work it into a balanced story, trying to guess whether her superiors at *Time* would let her go ahead with it once they learned where she was aiming. She told me that she'd felt a little like Woodward and Bernstein must have felt just before they broke the story of Watergate.

"Then they visited me," she said, her voice so soft I could barely hear the words. "I'll never forget that night. Two years, two months, and twenty nights ago. There were three of them. Two enforcers that looked enough alike to be twin brothers, and Rathjen."

"Rathjen himself, the head cheese of the Union?"

"Yes. You sound as if you don't believe me. I didn't believe my own eyes. I knew he couldn't be there in my apartment. He was in Europe all that month, lecturing to Drakean groups every day. The network news had carried a story on him just that evening, and there was live coverage of his tour every day on the Drake cable channel."

"The Union has a fleet of private jets," I reminded her.

"And no private airfield to land on," she said, "not on the East Coast anyway."

"Did he tell you how he pulled the trick?"

"He didn't speak until they were through with me," she said. "When he did talk, it wasn't about that. But it was Rathjen."

"Maybe he's like a movie star," I suggested. "A lot of them have stunt men and there's sometimes an amazing physical resemblance between the double and the star."

"Down to the exact same voice?"

I had heard Rathjen's voice on the tube now and then, as everyone in the United States had at one time or another, regardless of their Drakean affiliation. A deep hypnotic bass that could almost make you believe the earth was flat. But voices, and especially distinctive voices, can be imitated. Rich Little makes his living doing it, and I am modestly talented in the art myself. But telling Sarah that would have exposed more of me than I cared to bare, so I kept my mouth shut.

"Down to missing the top joint of his right forefinger?" she added.

This time I didn't know what to say so I kept quiet again, leaving the burden of continuing the dialogue on her.

"They woke up Cathy," she said. "They made her . . . made her watch." She broke again, couldn't go on for a while. "She was four years old. One of the twins put a handkerchief across her mouth and sat her on his lap and the other one made me take off my nightgown, and then we all just stood there and Rathjen kept staring at me as if my body disgusted him, and Cathy was sobbing in the enforcer's arms and they wouldn't let me go to her, and after what seemed like years they made me go down on my knees in front of Rathjen, and the other enforcer knelt behind me and held a butcher knife to my neck, and—I remember Rathjen was wearing a beautiful gray cashmere suit that must have cost thousands of dollars—and . . . and Rathjen unzipped his fly and they made me . . . made me do things to him, and he . . . he went in my mouth, and afterward when I was coughing and gagging on my knees the enforcer held a silk handkerchief to my mouth for me to spit it into, and then they made me wash out my mouth over and over and they wouldn't let me get dressed and go to Cathy until I had, and we were clutching each other and crying, and the enforcers separated us and took me over to Rathjen again, and I thought they were going to kill both of us, and that was when Rathjen spoke for the first time. He looked down at me like I was a worm, and he said: 'You will never talk about this to anyone.' And he made me repeat it on my knees in front of him. And he said: 'You will never talk or write of the Circle again.' And I had to repeat that too. And all the time he was looking across the room at Cathy, and he was still looking at her when he said: 'See that you keep your word.' And he didn't have to say that if I made them come back here again they'd do something unspeakable to my child, I got the message without his having to say a word. And then his men went through the apartment without leaving even the trace of a mess and found all the raw material for my story that I'd been keeping there and took it with them when they left. I couldn't go to work for a week. I called in sick, I was paralyzed with fright. When I could finally make it to the office, I was told that I was fired, and I found out that the editor who'd put me on the story was also fired. The material on the Union that I'd kept at the office was missing from my file drawer."

Something about her story and the almost narcotized way she told it crept into my bones, turned me into a ball of nerves. I kept flicking glances around the darkened room, seeing poison spiders in the shadows. I reached up and clicked on some more lamps. I wanted out of this damn case. I wanted to kill someone. I sat down next to her again and tried to make myself think rationally. It took a while. The silence in the room was like a fifth wall.

"They did all this to you," I asked her at last, "and you never made a squawk? Sued the magazine? Filed a rape charge?"

"If you'd been me, would you? My God, they were so careful, I couldn't even prove anything had happened to me! And if they ever came back . . ."

"You've kept all this buried inside for two years? Never told a woman friend, or your brother?"

"I've never told anyone," she said, "until tonight. Oh, God, I shouldn't have told you either!" She broke again, buried her face in her hands, shoulders quaking.

"They're all around us, everywhere, at the magazine, in the streets, in the police and the government, they'll get me for telling, they'll rape my baby . . ."

"The hell they will," I told her, and flung myself off the couch and crossed the room and tore the handset from the base of the phone and punched out the number of the Essex House Hotel. "Mr. Landy's room, please," I told the night operator. I counted the number of rings, seven, eight, nine, and was screaming to myself *Where the fuck is he?* when a sleep-sodden but unmistakably black voice mumbled into my ear a tentative hello.

"Landy?"

"Yeah, this is Landy."

"You know who this is?"

"I think so." The voice was alert and cautious now. "But why don't you make us both feel better and prove it?"

"We first met last week," I told him. "McGaughy was carrying a tan leather attaché case and you had a Magnum. We had lunch in the limo. Seafood pasta—"

"That's enough," he said. "How come you done woke me out of a sound sleep?"

"I want to find out how good a bodyguard you are. McGaughy said you're his top man."

"I'm the best," he said.

"That better not be bullshit," I said. "Get your pants and raingear on, grab a cab, and meet me in the Village." I gave him Sarah's address on West Twelfth Street, made him write it down. "Wait for me across the street, in front of The New School. I'll be bringing a woman with me. Your job is to be her guardian angel till I tell you otherwise."

"Hold still a minute, man," he said. "I don't take orders from you, only from Mac, and he told me to watch over you, not some chick you gone and picked up."

I started to seethe inside, came very close to cursing

him out over the phone, but controlled the impulse and shot a glance at the red-numeraled time readout built into the suite's TV. Few minutes after eleven. "Can you get hold of McGaughy and get his okay on this? It's really damned important."

He seemed to understand that it was, got dead serious all of a sudden. "Yeah, I can get hold of him," he said. "Give me five minutes. Where can I call you back?"

I gave him the Beverly number and the name I was using. Went back to the couch and sat and stared at the red numbers on the time readout. They seemed to have stopped moving. It took hours for them to go from 11:06 to 11:07.

"I remember something," Sarah said, watching me watch the motionless red figures. "The night they came for me, when they were gone I looked at the clock. Thirty-nine minutes. That's all the time it took them to tear me apart."

"They'll never come back," I told her, and took her frozen hands in mine. "You're safe now. You and Cathy are safe." I had never more fervently hoped I was telling the truth.

The phone rang. I caught it before the second ring and sure enough it was Landy. "Mac says it's okay," he said, "but only till you take off for that Monckton place. From then on you gotta get someone else to watch your lady."

"You know anyone as good as you?"

"Ain't no one as good as me," he said.

"I know some people who might be in your league," I told him. "But till morning, you're it. We'll see you in front of The New School at midnight." I hung up and crossed to the couch and reached out to help her to her feet.

"Time to go home," I told her. "You're protected from now on, believe me. All you need to do is go on about your normal life. People are going to be watching you, but they're all on our side. You'll be meeting one of them in a little while." I wondered how many other men and women in the media had been terrorized as Sarah had been, how many critical reports on the Union had been aborted. I wondered what had happened to the sources Sarah had interviewed before her thirty-nine-minute night with Rathjen. How many times must she have asked herself the same question? How deep was her sense of guilt for betraying to Rathjen's tender mercies the people who had confided in her? With that guilt reinforcing her abject terror, it was a miracle she hadn't killed herself by now.

We descended to the Beverly's petite but elegant lobby, nodded to the uniformed night attendant, and went out into the dripping darkness. I snagged us a prowling cab and gave him an uptown destination. No one was on our tail. We switched cabs at Park in the upper Eighties and streaked south to the Village. It was seven after midnight when the cab swung into West Twelfth. As the driver slowed in front of her building I caught a blur of trenchcoat on the other side of the street and felt an exquisite moment of nausea until the blur stepped under a light and I recognized the long beanpole body. When the cab was paid off and out of sight I guided Sarah across the pavement and into the recessed doorway of The New School and introduced her to her protector. For the first time in hours she smiled, just barely. In a few well-chosen words I outlined the situation for Landy. Then I took Sarah into her building and up in the elevator. We hugged in the corridor for a few seconds before she stuck her key in the lock. The only words she said were: "Thank you." I went down the street again and inconspicuously nodded good night to Landy and sauntered through the drizzle back to Sixth and another cab. No one was on our tail.

By one o'clock in the morning I was back at the

Beverly with the phone soldered to my ear, still playing Lattman the prince of PIs, arranging round-the-clock protection for Sarah Rogers to commence with the dawn. The firm with which I made arrangements calls itself New York Security. Its administrators and a few of its field people are full-timers but the vast majority are free-lance. The city is glutted with men and women who live for the big dream, the fantasy of fame and fortune as actors, dancers, models, whatever. Most make less from their chosen professions, or perhaps the word is obsessions, than they would on welfare. To augment their pitiful creative income, some wash dishes, some wait tables, some drive taxis, some do hooking. Those with experience in the cops or the military and those who look like Rams fullbacks usually sign on with New York Security. As Lattman I had used the firm time and again. The night manager promised me that Ms. Rogers and her daughter would be covered by seven in the morning.

It took four and a half days to finish my homework and close down my New York identities. I checked out of the Beverly, cabbed to my condo, packed my bags afresh, strolled across Fifty-Ninth to the Essex House Hotel and left a message in Mr. Landy's box—"See you in Monckton. Peter Porter"—and strolled back to the condo. I set the deadbolts, lugged my bags to the lobby, and caught a cab to La Guardia, where, under one of the paper and plastic personas I maintain for such occasions, I boarded a late afternoon TWA flight, whose terminus, after an intermediate stop in Chicago, was the city I was being paid one million dollars to visit.

6

I have become all things to all men, that I might by all means save some.

St. Paul, I Corinthians 9:22

VISUALIZE A CYLINDER twenty stories tall, its exterior formed of interlocking panels of mirror glass. Split the cylinder lengthwise, join the halves with a common base of steel and glass four stories high, add banks of glass-walled elevators that silently slither up and down the split sides. This is the Monckton Airhotel. It was my first stop after deplaning and plucking my bags off the luggage carousel. I took an escalator from the baggage claim area to the monorail platform, boarded the robot train that linked airport and hotel, exited three minutes later at an identical platform glistening in the starlight, escalatored down to the ground-floor reception lobby, and signed in. To the hotel and the world in general I was Peter J. Porter, investment consultant, of White Plains, New York. A bellhop escorted me up in one of the fishbowl elevators, set down my bags at the door of 1808, stuck a plastic card into a slot set in the door frame. The lock clicked open. The bellhop smiled and handed me the card, and I smiled back and handed him two bucks. I chain-locked the door and unpacked and showered and dropped into instant sleep. Next morning, accoutered in sportshirt, slacks, and a blazer, I descended to the lobby and patronized first the coffee shop and then the auto-rental desk. By nine-thirty I was enthroned behind the wheel of a steel gray Toyota Camry and pointed toward Monckton.

It is the king city of southwest Illinois, a hive of history and a maze of contradictions. The brochures in McGaughy's manila envelope had given me a bird's-eye view of its life. First platted by an Eastern land speculator in 1813, legally incorporated as a city twenty years later when its population hovered around four thousand. In the decades before the Civil War, a key station in the underground railway system that whisked runaway slaves north. During the war years, the site of a prison and hospital where thousands of Confederate prisoners lived in unspeakable filth and, if they were lucky, died. In the postwar boom decades, the age of gold for robber barons like Jim Fisk and Andrew Carnegie and Barnabas Drake, a bustling brawling city-on-the-march, with sand plants, steel plants, glassworks, flour mills, stone quarries, icehouses, and firearms factories, flourishing cheek by jowl with genteel little academies where young ladies were instructed in the duties and skills expected of them by God and their men. But Monckton was also a river city, a hub for the movement of people and produce, thanks to its location on the Mississippi. Hordes of freight and passenger boats steaming in and out of its docks. Huge levee, complete with switch track and three packet sheds, throbbing night and day in wheat and apple harvest time. There on the riverfront was where Drake made his pile, moving the goods off the steamboats and into his railroad cars and across the heartland, moving other goods out of the heartland and into his freight cars and across to the river ports. That world still flourished when Barnabas Drake experienced The Event, and still flourished in 1906 when he died. It's gone now, and just about everyone who was a part of it is dead. Classic Monckton consists of that world's ruins, each surviving rubble heap scrupulously enshrined in the National Register of Historic Places.

With maps and brochures on the passenger seat beside me I wove in and out through the center of the city, stopping on occasion to tour a few blocks on foot, to grab a burger at a corner cafe and skim the local paper over my second cup of coffee. Six hours of observant wandering and I'd seen enough of the seedy aimless side of contemporary Monckton to last a lifetime. Steep cobblestoned streets unfit for auto traffic, dried-up small businesses, ramshackle video stores, ugly brick apartment buildings, dim corner bars where the laid-off and the retired nursed beers through the endless afternoons and mumbled about their golden pasts. Such was downtown Monckton today. I didn't think it could have been much different twenty years ago, when a brilliant and lost young man in his teens wrote verses about mice eating the sacred cheese of love to a female classmate who preferred the captain of the fabled Wombats football eleven. That classmate was back in town now, residing at 5407 Sturges Place after an interval of marriage and widowhood in Lamoni, Iowa. She thought those mouse-and-cheese poems were worth two million dollars, and if they were genuine, she was probably underpricing them.

The other side of the Monckton coin was shiny with hope for the future. The airport, dating from when Federal money grew on trees. The space-station ambience of the Airhotel. The ring of executive office parks around the city's periphery. The multileveled shopping malls just off the interstates. The trendy *ristorantes* and fern-choked singles bars and the patches of Old Town, where yuppies had moved in and rehabbed. How much of the economic boom was connected with Union Island and

Barnabas Drake University? My brochures didn't say, but Drakeans were known for upgrading whatever they touched.

Deadheading back to the hotel, I shunned the direct route and detoured along the length of Sturges Place. It was a quiet street, maybe three-quarters of a mile from one end to the other, running through a still halfway decent district of sleepy old houses, their wide front yards dotted with majestic trees. Number 5407 was larger than its neighbors, a slate-roofed Tudor revival from the Twenties, off-white stucco with brick trim. I wondered why a woman on her own would lease a house so much larger than she was likely to need. As I drove by she was in the front yard, raking crisp dead leaves into heaps on the lawn. She looked up at the passing Camry and then down at the leaf mounds again. I made myself keep my eyes straight ahead but tilted the rearview mirror till it gave me a parting glimpse of her for a split second. All I gained from that was a sense that she looked like her photos, slender and fine-boned, dark hair pulled tight in a bun, and an impression from the precise pyramids of gold-red-brown leaves that she was a neatsy person. And the wheels of creativity started spinning in their unfathomable way, and before I was on the ramp to the Interstate I had the skeleton of a plan.

The bar in the vast open lobby of the Airhotel was awash with the happy-hour crowd when I passed through. A jazz pianist was tickling the ivories, but over the dull roar of customers no one could hear a note. The thirsty congregated at the horseshoe bar, the hungry around the buffet table with its chafing dishes full of hot munchies, the horny around the opposite sex. Cocktail waitresses in mauve velvet mini-dresses sashayed with drink trays from nook to nook. I scanned the sweet displays of breast and thigh and was just asking myself whether I dared seek out a bed buddy right here in my safe house when I saw a particular face at the buffet, bending over a saucerful of barbecued chicken wings, and my urge for amour was gone. *God damn it, how had he found me so soon?* With plate in hand the bright-eyed black beanpole kept his glance wandering through the mob as if he were waiting for his special lady and his eyes caught mine but he didn't stop searching, just nodded—or was that my imagination?—and set down his plate and drifted out of sight behind a knot of young execs in power suits. The whole silent encounter hadn't taken more than ten seconds. I kept moving across the lobby toward the bank of elevators, the back of my neck sensing him somewhere behind me. A steel cage door hissed open and the glass maw swallowed me, spitting me out at 18. The whitewalled tube of corridor was empty. I followed the pale blue carpeting to the door of 1808 and turned back toward the elevator fully expecting to see him loping along the hallway. It was still empty. But there was a dull burring sound from inside my room.

I stuck my entry card in the slot, banged the door shut, caught the phone in midring. "Yes?" I said cautiously.

"This Peter Porter I talking to?"

"Yes," I said even more cautiously, not certain of his voice.

"This is room service, man. What room you in?"

It was Landy all right, calling from a house phone downstairs. I hadn't expected him to find me so soon and my pride, not to speak of that sudden gnawing of sexual desire, made me wish I'd eluded him at least till morning. But in light of my inspiration on the hotelward journey, I needed him.

"Eighteen-o-eight," I sighed. "Come on up."

He was stretched out on one of the twin queen-size beds, jacket off, shoes off, bare toes wriggling happily, eyes glowing with satisfaction. "We was circlin' around and around and waitin' for the air traffic controller to let us land and every time I looked down at the ground out of my little plastic window I sees this science-fiction hotel alongside of the airport and I say to myself, That's the kind of place would appeal to him."

"True son of McGaughy," I said. In a blue-tufted wing chair I looked down through my own tinted window at the sun-bright pool on the roof of the hotel's central base, between the segments of cylinder and fourteen floors below me.

"So I take the robotmobile from the airport to over here, and I say to the clerk is a Peter Porter stayin here, and the clerk say yes he is, so I try to get Peter Porter on the house phone and they ain't no answer so I check in myself and call every half hour and then I drift down to the bar for happy hour and you know the rest. I'm in seven-forty-three. This pad's nicer." He crossed his ankles luxuriantly and reached for the water glass on the bedside table, which held no water but bourbon on rocks. "What you got for me to do?"

His grasp of the syntax of white English may have been faulty but that man could read me effortlessly just as his impish mentor could, and the pair of them frightened me. I tried to keep the unease out of my voice. "What sort of clothes did you pack?"

"Some of this, some of that. You never said how long we'd be here or what I'd need."

"Any street-dude outfits? Velvet hat, gold chains, cowboy boots, that kind of stuff?"

"You want me to look like some motherfuckin pimp?" he demanded in a tone seething with outrage.

"Right on," I told him, and unpocketed my wallet. "You can buy the props tonight if you don't have them."

"Mac don't like me to wear shit like that," he said. "*I* don't like me to wear shit like that."

"Why not?"

"Cause that's the shit I used to wear," he said quietly, "before Mac put my head on straight." He took a long pull at the bourbon, sat upright on the bed with the pillows against his back. "But maybe I'll do it if you say there's a reason."

"There is. I want you to spend a few days and nights in the combat zone. Roam the joints, spend money. Be cool. Listen much, say little. Find me some reliable local talent, four or five men. If you connect with one good guy he can probably put you in touch with the others."

"What kind of talent you got in mind? Legbreakers, heist men, shooters?"

"God, no!" I almost shouted at him. "No violence. Just guys who aren't too bright and will do what they're told if the money's right. Nothing too risky or illegal."

"You want black guys, white guys, or salt and pepper?"

"I couldn't care less," I announced in the best manner of the original liberals who fought and bled for the cause of a color-blind society, until their ideological children dreamed up affirmative action and smeared their forebears' dream as racist. "No, wait," I corrected myself, suddenly realizing that my plan, true to its time, demanded a racial quota. "Two blacks maximum, not counting yourself. The rest have to be white. And the whites have to be the sort you look at and don't remember. They have to blend with the scenery."

"You want me to put this team together in a couple days and nights?" His tone suggested that I had asked him to bring down the moon on wires.

"Take all the time you need," I said. "We're in no great rush. But whatever you do, don't mention me and don't come near me again till the team's ready to roll. Keep your room here but find a second place where you and the others can meet."

"When do they get to meet you?"

"They don't. As far as they're concerned, you're the honcho. In other words, they're the grunts, you're the field commander, and I'm the general in the Pentagon." The brightness snapped out of his eyes and was replaced by a cold tight murderous look. "Did I say something stupid?"

"Yeah," he said. "Don't you ever talk that military bullshit to me again."

"Okay if I ask why it bothers you?"

"I was a grunt once." His voice was stiff and dead. "Central highlands of Nam, 1968 and '69. I had to off a lot of people hadn't done me no wrong, old men, women, some kids. I left my manhood over there, and I brought back a heroin habit took me ten years to break. So no more military talk. Understood?"

"Whatever you say."

He thrust himself up from the bed and crossed the room barefoot to where my wallet lay on the table in front of me, helped himself generously to bills, and seemed to be daring me to stay his hand, which I chose not to try. "I'll call when it's lined up," he said, and, sticking his feet into his clodhoppers, his socks in his pockets, and his suit jacket under his arm, he opened the door a crack and peered out and made his exit. Without a smile or a wave or a good-bye. I seemed to have triggered memories in him that he could have lived without.

I was alone in the cool sterile room with only the hum of the hotel's invisible machinery for company. I thought about the happy hour still in session downstairs, and the pert breasts and tanned bare arms of the cocktail waitresses. *No,* the voice of prudence admonished, *this is your safe house. Keep it that way.*

I kicked off my own shoes, flung myself on the unmussed bed, and played with the plan in my mind. Adding a touch here and a refinement there, clothing the skeleton's bones with flesh. I didn't allow myself to go out for supper until I was honestly convinced that the crazy scheme more likely than not would work.

The next day I went house-hunting.

Hard autumn rainfall beat on the Camry's roof as I drove back to the residential district and made a slow systematic circuit of every block within a square mile of 5407 Sturges Place. A midget cassette recorder sat on the passenger seat within arm's reach. Whenever I saw a *For Sale By Owner* sign in the window of a house or on a frame thrust into a lawn, I reached for the recorder and flicked the button and dictated the number on the sign plus the address of the property and a brief superficial description. In the dreary rain it was slow going. I deliberately stretched it out over the day so that the Camry wouldn't be noticed too often, and once in a while when the precip seemed to be letting up I'd park on a side street and slip on raingear and cover part of the ground on foot. I had seventeen prospects by cocktail time.

That evening, which was too wet to venture forth in anyway, I stayed cooped up in room 1808, calling each of the day's harvest of numbers in turn, employing for each conversation a different voice from my repertoire. Twelve of the seventeen were in. Seven of the twelve I quickly ruled out: either their homes didn't have all the features I needed or they wouldn't consider a rental offer. Three of the remaining five sounded promising. At the end of the evening I called back and made appointments to inspect the trio next day.

The third house was made to order for me. Small, screened from its neighbors by shrubs, set back from the street, with an attached garage whose connecting door led straight into the kitchen so that anything brought into the place by auto would not be seen by the curious. The owner was a woman in her late sixties who had inherited it from her mother long ago. She had rented it out when she could to supplement her social security check, but the Illinois winters were too hard on her brittle bones, and she wanted to dump the place and move into her widowed sister's condominium in Fort Lauderdale. The house had been on the market for months without takers. I tendered the lady my Peter Porter card and explained that my specialty as an investment consultant was real estate. Computer analysis had convinced me that the next Monckton neighborhood in which rehabbing yuppies were likely to swarm would be hers. But computers are not infallible and my operating capital was limited. Suppose I offered to lease the house for six months, with the entire rent paid up front so she could forget the property for a while and spend the coming winter in the sun? The lease contract would include an option to buy at her price, with the proviso that if I should exercise the option, and then sell the house to someone else at a higher figure, one-third of the profit would go to her.

She sprang at the offer like a hungry lion at its lunch.

On the way back to the hotel I stopped at a pay phone and put in a long distance call to Chicago, to the office of a certain lawyer who owed Arthur Lattman a favor. The next morning I caught a commuter flight to the Toddlin Town, bought the lawyer a three-martini snack, kept my mouth tight as to why I was helping some clown named Porter to rent a house, and was back in the Airhotel before dark with the legal papers in my pocket. Three days later the owner was on her way to Florida, and I had exclusive access to a house less than five minutes' walk from the home of Constance Young.

While the old lady was moving out, I stayed more or less confined to the Airhotel. Sleeping late, swimming in the pool on the fourth-floor roof when the sun was warm, working out on the Nautilus equipment in the basement health club. Sitting in front of the tube and watching too goddamn many sitcom reruns. I wanted to hear from someone. The only people who knew where I was were Landy and McGaughy, and I didn't have the foggiest notion where either of them was or even if McGaughy was within a thousand miles of me, but I was so bored I wouldn't have minded hearing from people who weren't supposed to know I existed. Like the religious leader who had raped Sarah Rogers in New York the same night he was lecturing in Europe.

What had prompted me to think of him was music. There was a digital clock radio on the night table between the queen-size beds, and I was idly twirling knobs that fourth morning, hoping at best for an inoffensive easy-listening station, when to my blissful surprise I heard a string quartet playing Schubert's "Death and the Maiden." Classical music in Monckton! At the end of the piece the announcer declared in dulcet murmurs that I was tuned to WBDU, 90.0 FM, the voice of the Circle, the radio station of Barnabas Drake University. Then came the chime of the hour and the national news headlines. I was hoping for more classical music following the news, but the next item on the schedule, so the announcer informed his audience, was a lecture on "The Drakean Sexual Ethic" by none other than Dr. Joseph Rathjen, president of Barnabas Drake University and high ferio of the Drakean Union. "The lecture is being simultaneously telecast on DCN," said the announcer, and I had flicked on the room TV and found the channel for the Drake Cable Network and was treated for the next fifty minutes to both the sight and the sound of the enemy. He looked as he had in the photograph in the BDU Bulletin: tall, silver-haired, majestic. A more-than-worldly power seemed to radiate through his body, even when he gestured with his right forefinger and you saw from the missing top joint that he was after all a human being. His deep, vibrant, sensuous voice resonated in stereo around room 1808, through the TV speaker on one side of the room, and through the radio speaker on the other, a voice you almost literally couldn't refuse to heed, a voice that could almost make you believe the sky was bleu cheese. He had made millions of reasonably intelligent people believe all sorts of propositions equally absurd. Dostoevski's Grand Inquisitor said it best: mankind craves miracle, mystery, and authority. Rathjen doled out all three with a generous hand. While his lecture rolled on, I had to remind myself over and over of Sarah Rogers's story. How *could* that man with the aura of the more-than-human have terrorized her and so many others? It was only after he was off the air, and an old John Wayne movie was beginning on the DCN and a Shostakovich cello concerto on WBDU, that I could answer my own question.

The answer was: With the greatest of pleasure.

It was well after dusk and I was packing a few items in an overnight bag when the phone sounded. With a silent hallelujah I dropped the bag and scooped up the handset.

"That you?" It was Landy, cautious as ever. "Let's just make sure it you. Tell me what room I'm calling from."

The test did not strain my memory since I'd been buzzing his room four times a day for the past two days, hoping he'd call in for messages and then call me. "Seven-forty-three," I said.

"Be up in two minutes."

It took him almost ten, but who counts? This time he kept his shoes and socks on and sat on the bed's edge rather than sprawling all over it, but otherwise the scene was a replay of our first conversation in this room. He looked as if he might keel over any moment from sleeplessness, gulped straight bourbon as if it were water.

"I put in long hours," he said, "but I got what you

want. Five guys. One black, four white. Two of the whites be wanted locally, they tried to knock off the ticket office while the Monckton Wombats was playin their big game with the football champs from the next county. The other three be clean."

"Get rid of the two who are wanted," I told him. "Can you find one clean guy to replace them?"

Landy cupped his bearded lantern jaw in his hand, cogitating. "Seems to me one of the clean guys said he had a brother. But this brother may limp a little. Seems he busted a kneecap last month runnin' down some fire stairs when he had to leave a apartment in a hurry cause the chick's main man got home from work early."

"Sign him on," I said. "He won't have to walk much. Okay, that gives us you plus a crew of four. Keep them ready for action. Meanwhile, I've got another little chore for you."

"Hey, come on, man, I gotta sleep every few days!"

"This can wait awhile. You'll only have a few hours' notice when I want you to do it but it won't happen for one or two nights anyway. I want you to go into the black ghetto and bring me back a present."

"No," he said, and stood up and put his hands on his hips defiantly. "You ain't gonna have me steal from my own people. I did that when I was on coke but never again, not even if Mac tells me to do it, and I know he never would."

"It's not stealing," I told him. "I want you to bring me something they'd gladly pay you to take away."

A look of blank puzzlement crept into his fatigue-hooded eyes.

"Cockroaches," I said.

In the small hours, when the residential streets of Monckton were graveyard still, I cruised down Hunter Drive sans headlights and braked in the driveway of my newly rented abode, opened the garage door noiselessly, and eased the Camry in. I plugged in a tiny shielded nightlight—the utilities wouldn't be disconnected till the end of the month—and by its feeble glow I moved my stuff from the trunk into the house. A futon and thermal blanket for sleeping, a change of clothes, toiletries, a few frozen dinners, a jug of white wine, a portable radio with earphones so that no strains of music would reach the neighbors. Last but far from least, the handy-dandy illegal phone which is my regular traveling companion on jobs away from New York. Its name is Alfred. I used the last hour of darkness to hook Alfred into the house's deactivated wiring. Stifling yawns, I slipped away before the street began to stir and rode the empty interstate back to the Airhotel for a long and amply deserved nap.

For the next two days I played the shadow game. Total waste, crashing bore. I learned no more and no less than I already knew from the report of the Chicago peepers who had spent a week doing the same thing. Constance Young visited no one and had no visitors. She went out to shop and that was it. The rest of the time she holed up in her nest. What was she doing in there? What does anyone do who's alone in the world with endless time to kill? Read. Watch soaps and game shows and rented videos on the tube. Meanwhile I sat in the Camry, spying uselessly on 5407 Sturges Place, keeping my mind occupied by keeping the car radio tuned to WBDU. The ratio between classical music and Drakean exhortations seemed to be fifty-fifty. Once each day there was a talk by Rathjen, and three times each day there was a discourse on one or another Drakean topic by a speaker whom the announcer introduced as "Dr. Mark Dextraze, doctrinal colinory of the university community, voluant ferio of the Circle." That meant he was the man responsible for the orthodoxy of what was taught at BDU and the next in line to take over the supreme leadership of the

Drakean Union when Rathjen went senile or crapped out. The religion's esoteric jargon was one of the items I'd developed a nodding acquaintance with during my preparation time in New York. I didn't know what this Dextraze looked like, but his voice wasn't in the same universe with Rathjen's. When he got excited, he squeaked. I had a hard time visualizing him as the ultimate authority of a world-class religion, but in a perverse way it was fun to try. To such amusements I was reduced as my shadow days crept in their petty pace from hour to hour.

On the afternoon of the second day I saw what should have slapped me across the face on the morning of the first.

Constance Young spent most of her waking hours watching television. If she'd been living this way for months, she would probably have decided long ago that she needed the largest possible number of channels to choose from at any given moment. That meant she would probably have subscribed to the cable service. I knew that cable was available in the area, thanks to having watched Rathjen on the Drake Cable Network from the hotel, but I didn't know for sure that Young was a cable subscriber. If she was, I knew what to do. I gave up my watch on the house, drove down streets speckled with red and gold and brown from fallen leaves, let myself into my home away from home on Hunter Drive, sat Japanese style on the living room floor, and lifted faithful Alfred to my lap.

After three rings I was rewarded with a ghastly high-pitched chirp in my ear. "Midcontinent Cablevision, good afternoon!"

In my busy life there are times when I must persuade someone at the far end of a telephone line that I am a member of the sex into which I was not privileged to be born. For this reason I keep a small supply of female tones in my voice repertory. I activated one of them now. "This is Mrs. Young," I told the chirp, "at 5407 Sturges Place. I have a question about my last bill."

"Just a moment, please, I'll transfer you," sang the receptionist bird, and the chirp was replaced by a snatch of canned music and then by another woman's voice, older, gruffer. "Accounts Department, Wilson."

"This is Mrs. Constance Young, 5407 Sturges Place. I have a question about my last bill."

I heard the unmistakable soft click of keys on a video display terminal being punched and could almost see the Wilson woman squinting at the printout of the Young account on her screen. Then I heard the gruff voice again. "Ma'am, your bill went out as usual on the twentieth of last month, and we received your check on the fourth of this month. I don't see anything here to question."

That was all I wanted or needed to know, and I could and perhaps should have hung up without further ado, but I had no desire to risk a return call from the company to the real Mrs. Young, so I was more or less obligated to improvise a question. "Err, yes," I replied. "The, ahh, the reception on my set was very poor for two days last month, and I was wondering if I could deduct the two days from my next month's bill."

"That's not my department," growled Wilson. "I'll give you the number of the Customer Relations Office." For which favor I thanked her more warmly than the old grouch deserved, and hung up.

I pressed the readout button on my watch. 3:26 P.M. Still enough time left on this bright crisp day to move on to the next step of the plan. I hunted through the phone directory graciously left behind by my landlady and found the address of Midcontinent Cablevision and located it on my Monckton street map.

The shank of the business day I spent parked inconspicuously across the highway from the cable company's HQ, watching their service vans come and go, eyeballing the work uniform their technicians wore on the job, snapping a few pictures with a midget Instamatic when no one was looking.

That evening, after a solitary meal in the Airhotel's rooftop eatery, I phoned Landy's room and as luck would have it found him in. "Caught up on your sleep yet?. . .Fine. Come on up, I've got a job for your crew." We were in conference ten minutes later. This time he sat up straight in a chair with his elbows on the Formica-topped dining table by the picture window. I handed him the shots of Midcontinent vans and green-overalled troubleshooters.

"That's all I want. Buy me a uniform like these, iron on the company's insignia. Rent a van of that make and color, paint the sides so any witnesses will think it belongs to the company."

"Save time and money we just borrow a real van while it's on a house call," Landy said. "We rent a van, we gotta paint it, then we gotta unpaint it before we turn it in."

"This is not a daredevil stunt we're pulling," I told him. "We do this safe and legal while we can. You've got the weekend to line it up for me, and that includes the roaches. Call me here at nine tomorrow evening, let me know how you're doing. Monday morning we roll."

"This is crazy, man," he grumbled. "I better call Mac, make sure he want me to do all this weird shit."

"McGaughy? Where is he? Is he in Monckton? Why the hell hasn't he been in touch with me?"

"He be around," Landy said. "I talked to him last night."

"Around *where?*

"I can reach him when I have to," Landy said, in a

tone that said for him, without his having to speak the words: And you can't.

I sensed something going on between the strange old white man and the strange young black man that I'd never understand. When I am working, anything I can't understand might kill me. On the other hand, I had no good reason for wanting to talk to the invisible gnome just then. But knowing he was both nearby and inaccessible somehow made me feel out of control, manipulated, powerless. I shrugged off the feeling as nonsensical. "Say hello to the old boy for me," I said.

"I hope you know what you doin'," he muttered dubiously, and kicked back his chair and drifted out of the room without ceremony.

"Me, too," I said, when he was safely out of earshot.

The next day, which was a Saturday, I drove out to the largest shopping mall in the county, a multileveled indoor labyrinth complete with escalators, ornamental fountains, acres of tiled floor, rest pits adorned with leather couches, skylights, hanging plants in abundance, a jazz pianist, and a Drakean *convul,* which is like a Christian Science reading room but more splendiferous, and well over a hundred cutesy little stores cunningly designed to part the consumers from their cash. I dropped into the sporting goods and hardware emporiums and made a few casual purchases I expected would soon come in handy. Wandered through the B. Dalton and Waldenbooks outlets, browsing through volumes on the subject of cable television. Took my evening meal in the food hall on the mall's lowest level, where ethnic takeout counters were arranged in a horseshoe around a central seating area the size of a football stadium. The temptation to eat silly was more than I could resist. I had a Greek salad, a bratwurst sandwich, a bottle of Japanese beer, a cream cheese brownie, and espresso. Afterwards I had the runs.

By nine I was back in room 1808, somewhat the worse

for my choice of cuisine, shoeless and sockless and propped up in bed with a glass of Pepto-Bismol on the night table and Prokofiev's *Scythian Suite* thundering over WBDU. When the phone rang, at seven past the hour, I flicked down the volume knob on the clock radio and reached for the handset. "You can pick up the shit any time you like," Landy told me without enthusiasm.

"The roaches too?"

"Wrapped up neat in a candy box," he said.

"And McGaughy said it was all right?"

"He said you know what you doing." He recited an address, which I took down on a sheet of Airhotel notepaper. I recognized the name of the street as an undesirable one near the riverfront. "You want to come meet me tomorrow?"

Tomorrow was Sunday. Suddenly as I lay there with the pillows supporting my neck I was seized with the burning desire to devote the next day to religious pursuits. And since Landy had already completed the chores I'd given him, there was no reason he couldn't keep me company. "No," I told him. "You come out here, say at nine-thirty in the morning. We're going to do some—" I was about to say reconnaissance and then remembered that was a military word. "We're going to take a day trip."

"Where we goin'?"

"To Union Island," I said.

The Camry bore us west through the bright crisp morning along Illinois Route 3, otherwise known as the Great River Road. Health nuts in down jackets and leg warmers pedaled furiously along the bike trail that ran parallel with the highway. Landy's eyes darted from the tugs and barges and pleasure boats dotting the brown Mississippi on our left to the harsh gray majesty of the towering bluffs on our right. For safety's sake I kept my eyes on the road.

"Hey, man!" He let out a whistle of astonishment and

pointed up at the top of the bluffs. "Look at that big old bird!"

"Chalked on the top of the cliff?" I said. "That's the Piasa Bird. It's an old Indian legend. They say the bird's a man-eater."

"You believe the legend?"

"I don't believe any legend," I said.

We slid past the turnoff to Barnabas Drake University, a system of gates and fortified guardposts that somehow reminded me of Checkpoint Charlie, between East and West Berlin. Beyond the junction of the Mississippi and the Illinois a line of interconnected paved lots at least half filled with parked cars took up the strip of land betweeen the road and the river. Passenger vans, painted blue and royal purple, roamed through the lots, dropping and picking up customers at designated loading points. "We're getting close," I said, and swung left into the next lot we passed, and wove through the aisles till I found and seized a vacant space. We paid the attendant, a tall pimply-faced girl with a blue-and-royal purple jacket on whose breast was the sign of the egg, and trotted through the chilly sunshine to where a queue of pilgrims stood waiting patiently at the ferry slip for the docking of the next boat. They were as quiet as a convention of deaf mutes. Most of their faces were alight with awe, the way I imagine the faces of Muslims must look when they first see Mecca. I adjusted my expression to match theirs and was about to motion to Landy to do likewise when I looked up into his eyes and saw that with him pretense was hardly necessary. The awe on his puss was real.

The long flat ferry churned through the muddy river and pulled into its slip, disgorging a throng of outward-bound travelers and then loading the next consignment, which included Landy and me. We crossed the steel gangway amid the silent horde and found standing room at the shoulder-high safety rail as the ferry hooted mournfully and whipped up the dark water into a froth, thrusting across the river to the other side, the holy side. Ten minutes later we merged into the hundred-odd men and women and children who exited the boat and marched across gravel to the starting point of the electrified tram line. We poured ourselves into two glass-walled cars as long as gondolas and took our places on hard seats cushioned in the Drakean colors of blue and royal purple. Golden sparks shimmered along the wires as the tram propelled us through the woods, with a toy house or outbuilding popping into sight every few moments in the far distance and then vanishing again. Squealing and hissing sparks, the tram swerved north, up the center of the tongue of land that had been a peninsula until the early 1920s, when the Drakean Union had bought or pushed out the farmers and dredged a channel across the northern end of the tongue and let the river fill its banks, literally isolating the place, turning it into an island. Landy sat staring at the countryside through the picture window like a hungry kid looking into the window of a candy store on Christmas Eve. On this part of the island the tram line was flanked by building complexes, impersonal brick high rises and low squat structures of brick and opaque glass, all of them shaped like eggs. People were moving about in the spaces between buildings, but all of them moved on foot, never in vehicles, which were verboten on Union Island unless you were a ferio. A blend of travelogue and religious sermon blared out from the tram's intercom. The ride to the terminus took twenty minutes.

We stepped out with our fellow visitors onto a concrete pad surrounded by buildings that formed an oval around the tram station. At least five hundred people were circulating this way and that way through the plaza, pouring in and out of the Drakean museum and the

Drakean gift center and the Drakean bookshop and the convul, or meditation hall, and the cafeteria and the rest rooms. Landy and I mingled with the herd, wandered through each building in turn. In the museum we were treated to a canned lecture which, thanks to the homework I had done in New York, taught me nothing about Drakeanism that I didn't already know. Afterward Landy wandered off on his own and I dropped into the bookshop, a high airy establishment stocked to the rafters with Drakean literature. Three display tables were piled with copies of a hefty volume entitled *A New Synthesis of the Godful World of Barnabas Drake*, which had been written by a savant named Gideon Mastrezat. Printed placards informed the curious that Dr. Mastrezat would give a public lecture in the auditorium of the main library of Barnabas Drake University on Tuesday evening, and afterward would autograph copies of his monumental tome. The better to blend with the crowd, I bought one for the discount price of $37.50. With the book conspicuously under my arm I sauntered out of the plaza and followed signs to the stone staircase cut into the side of a steep hill, at whose peak was the highest point on the island, from which one could look down upon the beating heart of the Circle and be glad, like Moses seeing the promised land. I reached the top and there, bending over one of the coin-fed binocular units rooted in concrete along a viewing platform, was Landy. I dropped two quarters into the machine next to his and twirled the focus knob. Into my vision it came, the headquarters, the hub, the pulsing center of the Circle, four concentric concrete oval buildings interconnected by short straight corridors, probably at least two miles from where we stood but huge and massive in the eyepiece as if they were only a few yards away. Somewhere in that labyrinth sat Dr. Rathjen, the high ferio. Somewhere else sat Dextraze, the voluant ferio, and a host of colinories and azanas and orents and all the other eccentrically dubbed ranks in the Drakean hierarchy. The place gave me an ache in the eyeballs.

"We going down there?" Landy spoke in barely above a whisper and kept his nose pressed against the cold steel of his machine.

"We don't have the ID," I whispered back. "That place is worse than Fort Knox. Besides, what would we learn?"

"I want to see what it like in there some day," he said.

"You could always become a Drakean," I told him. "Work your way up the ladder. Maybe make orent in ten years. Hell, if they have affirmative action you could make it in four or five."

"Fuck that shit," he said softly. Not being sure if he meant affirmative action or the Drakean religion, I glanced around me in a tremor of apprehension and made sure no pious ear had overheard. What did he think went on behind those walls? Wild sex orgies, drums and drugs and communal orgasm? More likely all he'd find if he ever made it into the heart of the Circle was the quiet sounds of a business tending to its business. Of midlevel management munchkins turning the pages of the Wall Street Journal, of computer printers spewing out data sheets, of accountants totting up columns of figures on their calculators. The sounds heard within the walls of General Motors and General Mills and Chase Manhattan and Omnitron and every other large corporation in the country. Why an honor grad of the school of the street would be turned on by such a prospect was way beyond my ability to fathom. I just couldn't understand the man.

We shared a bland and overpriced lunch at the Drakean cafeteria, and joined the line for the outward-bound tram and caught the ferry back to the mainland. By four-thirty we were in the stream of traffic heading east on the river road and an hour later, having dropped Landy at the waterfront garage, I was in the heart of Monckton's residential district with a gaudily wrapped candy box on the passenger seat beside me.

For the evening and the first part of the night, the house on Hunter Drive was my home. I curled up on the futon a little after eight and was buzzed awake at two in the morning by my wrist alarm. In dark turtleneck and jeans and Reeboks I slipped out into the night and thanked the clouds for blocking the light from the moon. An alley brought me to the rear of 5407 Sturges Place. I crossed the back yard in an infantry crawl and buried myself in tree shadows, listening. The house was dead, the block was dead, the only sound was the crickets. I crouched in the shadows and counted slowly to one thousand. Nothing stirred. I took the night glasses purchased at the mall from the shoulder bag bought at the same shop, adjusted the focus knob, stared through the eyepiece at magnified stucco walls. Thanks to my bookstore browsing, I knew cable wire when I saw it. There it was, clinging to the east wall, held in place by staples driven into the stucco, then soaring across the yard to the nearest telephone pole. They must have drilled a hole in the wall to connect the wire with the TV, but I couldn't spot it.

I slithered from the tree shadows to the corner of the sleeping house and unsheathed the cutter from the mall's hardware store and snipped the wire twice. I crawled back to the shadows, caught up on my breathing, and scuttled into the alley and away. A cop car was prowling down Hunter as I turned the corner. I ducked behind a hedge and froze and tightened my bladder muscles. The ruby glow of the patrol car's taillights thinned to dots and winked out. Thirty minutes after the close encounter I was on my futon, groping for sleep.

A few minutes before nine the next morning, a teal

blue Econoline van with *Midcontinent Cablevision* on its side panels braked beneath the elm in front of 5407 Sturges Place. A tall handsome workman in the cable company's green coveralls emerged from the driver's door with tool kit in hand and sauntered up the flagstoned walk and rang the bell. I ought to know. The workman was me.

It took a while to rouse her. Instinct told me she was at an upstairs window out of my line of sight, peering down at the company logo on the van. I waited a full minute between rings, but I did keep ringing. There was the clack-clack of shoes on uncarpeted staircase and floor, the heavy oak door swung back, and there she was, framed in the storm door's glass. My target, close up for the first time.

Face to face she looked better than in the photos from the peepers, her hair softer, her features less severe. She wore a blue oxford cloth shirt and a pullover sweater and jeans. I tried my damndest to keep my face devoid of interest.

"Miz Young?" I used my high-school-dropout mumble.

She stood there motionless and unsmiling, made no move to open the storm door between us.

"I'm with Midcontinent, ma'am. Our monitoring equipment tells us there's a mal . . ."—true to my role I stumbled over the word—"a malfunction in the wiring somewhere around here. Ma'am, have you turned on your set this morning?"

"Not the one connected to the cable," she said, her voice low and precise like a schoolteacher's. "Just the small set in the kitchen that I watch the morning news on while I'm having breakfast."

"Would you mind turning on the set that's cable-connected? Just for a minute, ma'am." I offered her a hesitant smile.

"Of course." No smile in return. "Wait here, please."

She shut the oak door, and I heard the rattle of the lock being set. This lady was no fool when it came to admitting strangers to her house. The clack of her footsteps receded and two minutes later returned. She unlocked the door and opened it and this time she opened the storm door too. "You're right," she said, chewing on a sliver of lower lip. "I tried all the channels and I can't get anything on the set at all except static."

"I think I can fix it for you, ma'am. If you'll let me in for a minute? Could be the connection came loose or something." I flashed her another of my gawky smiles. "There won't be a charge for the call, ma'am," I added.

The surest way to breach someone's defenses is to offer a service for nothing. Mrs. Young hesitated a few seconds while frown lines momentarily scarred her forehead, but then she stood aside and let me in. We walked down a long glistening hardwood-floored hall with a marble staircase curving up at the left, and turned right at an archway, stepping into a high-ceilinged living room with fake Oriental rugs underfoot, mismatched chairs and tables and lamps scattered about, a few paintings of motel-room quality on the wall. It would have looked like a room no one ever lived in except for the cat, a lean young black kitty with snow-white feet who lay curled on the seat cushion of one of the chairs with its head tucked between its front paws, pretending to be asleep. When I came into its ken the cat gave a lazy stretch and bounded to the carpet and began rolling playfully on its back, mewing for attention. I am a sucker for cats. I went down on one knee, chucked its chin and rubbed its belly and let it rub its sandpapery tongue on my forefinger.

"His name is Jim Socks." Mrs. Young smiled. "I got him from the local Humane Society when I moved here. He's wonderful company but please don't indulge him too much, he'll keep you petting him for hours."

I read in her voice that the lady and I were not quite

strangers anymore, and that was good; I had to make her trust me in a hurry. I treated Jim Socks to a final caress on his forehead, sighed, and got to my feet and went over to the household appliance that was my excuse for being here. The TV was angled against the junction of two walls, a 25-inch model on a sturdy wheeled table with a VHS videorecorder on its lower shelf and a neat row of cassettes on its upper shelf—*And Justice for All, Sudden Impact, Annie Hall, Vertigo*—and a maze of wires tangled helter-skelter between the two pieces of electronic hardware. One wire ran from the rear of the TV to a hole drilled in the wall. That had to be the cable. Knowingly I squatted down by the set and started to fiddle with the control buttons and fondle the wiring. Understandably enough, the set emitted neither picture nor sound and not even white noise.

Everything hung on the next sixty seconds. I took an unobtrusive breath, picked up my tool kit, and turned to face Mrs. Young, who was sitting on a chesterfield watching me as if I were her favorite morning talk show.

"Ma'am," I announced, "I need some more tools I got out in the van. Back in a minute." While saying the words I was moving steadily but not too speedily towards the archway to the hall. If she stood up and came over to make sure I went nowhere but out to the street, bang went the plan. My brain ordered my body to pay no attention to her. Her legs stirred and for a fraction of a second my heart stopped. Then she relaxed and settled herself more comfortably. Without breaking stride I sailed through the archway, out of her line of vision, and down the long hall to the front door.

At most, I had twenty seconds for the next step.

Keeping on the move the whole time, I unlatched the tool kit with one hand, pulled out the plain white candy box within, and raised the lid. A squad of cockroaches dived out of the candy box quick as lightning and streaked for the walls and the foot of the stairs and any crack in the wainscoting they could find. "SHIT!!" I screamed as loud as I could, and hurled the tool kit on the floor and kicked and mashed at the fleeing monsters with my thick-soled work shoes, cursing with the furious disgust of one for whom a roach is the obscenity of the earth. If I didn't zap at least one of them, bang went the plan again. I stamped and kicked like a madman and felt a squashing beneath my sole. "Gotcha!" I said almost out loud, and was scraping the remains off the bottom of my shoe with a piece of tissue when Mrs. Young and the cat came running frantically into the hall to see what the hell was happening. The whole operation had taken a quarter of a minute.

"I'm sorry, ma'am," I told her, rising from my squat. "Looks like you've got more than a problem with the TV. I came out here and saw a bunch of roaches and I just went crazy, I hate those things, they make my skin crawl."

"Oh, God," she said softly. "I've never seen a roach here before."

"You don't usually find them roaming around in broad daylight like that," I told her. "I'm no expert but that probably means you've got a big colony of them living between the walls and they're hungry." Now came the punch line. I took another breath. "If I were you, ma'am, I'd call an exterminator right away and have the place thoroughly sprayed."

She hesitated a beat, then edged along the hall toward me and stared repulsed at the gooey remnants of the one roach from the candy box who had paid Darwin's price for being just a shade slower than his brothers and sisters.

"Is your house protected by a year-round contract with an exterminating company, ma'am?" I inquired helpfully.

"No, I . . . I just rent the . . . the house, I've only . . . only lived here six months and never had this problem. You're right, though, I should call an exterminator now."

"That's a good idea, ma'am," I said, and stooped to retrieve my tool kit. "I'll go get the other things I need." And just as if nothing unsettling had happened I proceeded at a casual pace the rest of the way down the hall and through the oak door and out to the curb. Behind the shelter of the van I tossed the candy box into the rear compartment, then jogged briskly back to the house with tool kit in hand. The timing had to be right. I had to be bending over the set again when she made her call.

Luck of the Turners. On my re-entry the cat was gone and she was seated at a tall secretary desk with the Monckton Yellow Pages open on the blotter in front of her. I passed close enough to make out the heading *Pest Control Services*. She seemed stunned by the profusion of bug catchers in the listing. I squatted down by the TV with my back to her and resumed my pointless fumbling with the wires and acted like a workman totally oblivious to what the lady of the house was doing by the phone. But my ears were on the *qui vive,* poised for the click of the handset being lifted. The instant I heard it, I reached for my coverall's breast pocket and flicked on the microcassette recorder hidden in an empty cigarette pack and shifted on my haunches so I and the unit's microphone half-faced her. Across the large room I couldn't see what touchtone buttons she pressed, but I could make out their *deep-deep-dip-dip-doop-doop-deep* and when someone picked up on the other end I could of course hear her share of the dialogue clear as a bell.

"This is Mrs. Young at 5407 Sturges Place. I seem to be having a serious roach problem. Could you send out an exterminator right away, please . . . Not until tomorrow? . . . Well, if that's the quickest you can . . . I understand. What time tomorrow? . . . Ten o'clock will be fine but please make it sooner if you can, I'm here all day . . . Thanks so much."

I waited a few minutes after she had hung up before giving a sigh of defeat and throwing tools back into my kit and hoisting myself upright. "I don't think the problem's in here, ma'am," I said. "I'd better check the outside line." Once again I sauntered nonchalantly out of the room and down the hall, but this time I didn't beeline for the van. I strode through the neatly mown zoysia grass of her front lawn and did a left face at the corner of the house and found the hole in the stucco that I hadn't been able to spot with my night glasses, the one through which the cable exited the living room. I paced the length of the east wall, eyeballing the wire each step of the way, until with a whistle of discovery I halted and peered down at the slashes I had inflicted on the cable with my cutter less than eight hours before. I made a half turn toward the front of the house, and there she was at the head of the narrow strip of walkway, watching me again. "Come here, ma'am," I called. She quickstepped down the path to where I stood holding out the wire.

"Someone cut your cable, ma'am," I told her, then, lowering my voice to a near whisper like a conspirator in a bad movie, "Are there any teenagers in this neighborhood?"

"Not that I—"

"Vandalism like this is usually kids' work. Ma'am, I don't have the equipment to repair this, but I'll report it to the office right away and they'll have a specialist out here before you know it. Will that be okay?"

"I suppose it will have to be," she said, and gave a helpless rueful laugh. "Oh, God, what a morning! First Jim Socks threw up, then the roaches, and now this. What's going to come at me next?"

"Bad things hit close together sometimes, ma'am," I

replied with the air of a proletarian Socrates, "but good things do too. I . . . guess I better head back for the office and write up a report on this." As I sidled past her on the walkway I made a move as if I were about to give her a brotherly embrace and then a move back as if I'd decided it might be misunderstood. "I'm truly sorry about your troubles, ma'am," I said to her. "And I love your cat."

"Thank you," she said. "You've been very nice."

As I piloted the van away from the curb and into the empty center of Hunter Drive and away, I caught her reflection in the outside mirror. She was standing in the middle of the street looking after me. Memorizing the license plate number? That made me shudder even more than carrying a boxful of roaches had done. If she recognized either me or the van the next time we called at her house, there went the ball game.

On my way back to the riverfront parking garage, where I'd left Landy and the Camry and picked up the coveralls and the van, I made a pit stop at a drugstore and used the pay phone to put in a call reporting the cut wire to Midcontinent Cablevision in what this time was a more than passable imitation of the voice of Constance Young.

By ten-thirty the van and its contents were back in the parking garage, and I was in my own clothes and once again in the empty house on Hunter Drive, asprawl on the futon with the Monckton Yellow Pages under my nose. No wonder, I thought, that Mrs. Young had been taken aback on opening her copy of the same pages. Under Pest Control Services the book listed seven solid columns' worth of debugging establishments.

Which of those dozens of insect liquidators had she chosen? While she was on the phone, I had toyed with the notion of sparing myself an onerous and uncertain chore by the simple device of asking her which company she'd called. The voice in my head had told me No. Wouldn't be in character for a TV repairman, might arouse her suspicion. Better do it the hard way.

So there I sat on the futon, suffering through my task. First I depressed the Play button on the microcassette recorder, listened to the seven notes of the touchtone buttons she had hit. *Deep-deep-dip-dip-doop-doop-deep.* Then I lifted faithful Alfred's handset and pressed the tones for A-1 Exterminators, the first name in the listing, and listened to the ensuing sounds with the concentration of a *New York Times* music critic. *Deep-dip-doop-doop-dip-dip-dip.* Wrong number. I hung up before anyone could come on at the other end, rewound the cassette tape, played it again to refresh my aural recollection, then tapped out on Alfred the number of AAA Professional Pest Control. *Doop-doop-doop-doop-deep-dip-deep.* Wrong number. Hang up. Rewind cassette. Play again. And thus I slogged my way through the numbers of Abbco Pest Prevention, Allgone Pest Control, Apache, Atlas, Bee & Flea, Brite Pest, Bugs-Be-Gone, Bugs Burger, Chek-Pest, and dozens of less colorful business names. It took me almost an hour to cover three columns. I had become bored and disgusted and more than half certain that just to spite me she had chosen X Terminators Co., the last name in the listing, when there it came in my ear.

Kilkenny's Killabug. *Deep-deep-dip-dip-doop-doop-deep.* Voila! Eureka! Bingo! By this point in the routine those sounds were as familiar to me as the opening notes of Beethoven's Fifth Symphony, but to make assurance doubly sure I played the cassette again and tapped out the Kilkenny number again. Yes. Infallibly, unmistakably yes. I would have staked my freedom on it. Which, in a sense, I was.

The third and last time I called that number, I didn't immediately hang up but kept the handset to my burning ear, waiting for the sound of a human voice at the other end. Five rings, a click, and then in an old man's feeble whine: "Kilkenny's, g'morning."

"This is Mrs. Young," I said into the mouthpiece in my closest approximation yet to the calm sweet voice of that lady, "at 5407 Sturges Place. I called before about roaches in my house."

The thunder of the receiver being ungently set down exploded in my ear, and I heard the rustle of paper that suggested that the old geezer was consulting a work schedule. "Yes, ma'am," he wheezed when he came back on the line, "you're booked for ten tomorrow morning, says here."

"I'm cancelling that," I told the senior. "I've found another exterminator who can come out today."

"Righty ho, ma'am," he said, unfazed by the loss of a customer. Whoever the ancient was, he didn't seem to own the company. "I'll cross you off our books. Sorry it didn't work out."

"I'm sorry too. Have a nice day," I added, before he could offer that ubiquitous bromide to me, and hung up, but just for long enough to get a dial tone. Then I tapped out the numbers of the house on Sturges Place. When she picked up and said: "Hello," in a voice which to my unbiased ears was indistinguishable from my own pastiche, I responded in a neutral business tone she would never recognize again.

"Mrs. Young? Mrs. Constance Young, please?"

"This is Mrs. Young."

"Carl Oringer, ma'am, from Kilkenny's Killabug. Got good news for you, ma'am. You did say you'd like us to do you as soon as possible, right?"

"Yes, I did. Can you—"

"We've just had a cancellation, ma'am. We can fit you in this afternoon if you're sure you'll be home."

"Why, that's *very* good news! Yes, I can arrange to be home if you'll give me an idea what time to expect you."

I knew that question would be coming and I knew that

my answer, whatever it was, would be a wild stab in the dark. Another van, a mess of real and phony extermination gear, work outfits, the crew, travel time from our staging area in the riverfront parking garage to the residential suburb that was our target. And if my digital readout was to be trusted, it was already twenty before noon.

"How about four o'clock?" I said.

"Four o'clock will be fine," she replied.

Fine for her, anyway. For me it would entail almost four and a half hours of sheer pandemonium and jangled nerves as I tried to pull the act together. But I consoled myself with the thought that I had a fudge factor in my favor. No homeowner ever expects a contractor to be on time. Even if I were half an hour late, this lady desperately wanted me, or more precisely she wanted the bug man she thought I was.

"A truck and a full crew will be at your house around four," I promised her. "Thanks again for calling Kilkenny, ma'am."

Once again I hung up just long enough for the dial tone to resume, then I made my last call of the morning, to the pay phone in the seedy tavern near the riverfront parking garage where Landy was supposed to be waiting for me. Four rings and a low voice said: "Yeah?" The hours of doop-doops and deep-deeps had so frazzled my eardrums that I couldn't be sure it was he.

"What's your room number at the Airhotel?" I demanded.

"Seven-forty-three," he said. "What's yours?"

"Eighteen-o-eight, smartass. Now listen up," I told him. "We roll this afternoon. Get the cable company logo off the van, take the van back where you got it, and bring back another. Some different color, I don't care what as long as it's not conspicuous . . . No, we don't need a company logo this time . . . Because this time we're exterminators. When a homeowner in a nice neighborhood has an insect problem he doesn't want to broadcast the news, so a lot of exterminators use plain vans without insignia. . . Get your team together. Make sure they all have identical work uniforms. Go to a supply house and buy half a dozen drums of insecticide and spraying equipment. I'll meet you all at the parking garage at . . . let's say three-fifteen. And remember, I'm just a pickup you met at a bar and hired for this masquerade. When the job's over, you pay off the team and get rid of the props and close down the operation. I'll call you at the Airhotel when I can. Clear . . . ? Good luck, man. Go."

7

Long is the night to him who is awake.

The Dhammapada, V:1

AT TWELVE MINUTES past four that mild and breezy afternoon, an unmarked van, its tan exterior streaked with road dirt and rust, swung off the main boulevard into Sturges Place, slowed to a crawl after a few blocks as the driver poked his head out the window to read house numbers, and shuddered to a stop at the curb in front of a certain domicile built of stucco with brick trim. As the Volkswagen in the circus disgorges clowns, the van disgorged half a dozen men in deep green work pants and matching shirts with random names stitched in red above the breast pockets. Two of the six were black, one of these being the beanpole foreman of the crew. Of the four whites on the team, two looked enough alike to be brothers and one was a hulking youth with a beer gut and a face full of acne. The last and I hoped least conspicuous of the Caucasians was a certain Milo T., transformed by cheek pads and bushy mustache from all resemblance to the garrulous TV repairman who had visited this same abode earlier in the day. All six of us marched up the flagstone walk to the front door of 5407, brandishing what would pass among the uninitiated for exterminating gear. Landy pressed the bell. This time the lady of the house didn't run upstairs for a peek out the window before opening. The thick oak door swung back and Jim Socks bolted out between her legs into the front yard and rolled around on his back in the grass. My eyes darted for an involuntary moment to the cat and I made myself not think of what havoc the little beast could wreak if he recognized me.

I turned my eyes back to Constance Young, standing on the threshold in the same oxford cloth shirt and pullover and jeans she'd worn for my previous visit. She still looked gravely beautiful in a remote and detached way, but the welcome evaporated from her eyes and became a gawk of amazement when she saw the platoon of workmen on her doorstep.

"Miz Young?" said Landy, the first time I had heard him trying to sound deferential.

She seemed a tad hesitant to admit her identity, stood there swaying slightly, a puzzled frown forming above her brows. "Yes," she replied at last.

"We're Kilkenny's," he announced with a ring of pride. "We use our head and we kill bugs dead!" The line had not been rehearsed. I deduced that Landy had become possessed by the spirit of his role.

"My God," she said, "does it take so many of you to do one house?"

"It's the newest concept in pest control," he said. "Saturation technique. No way we miss a single place they hiding with all of us huntin' 'em out." He gestured toward where the cat was cavorting on the grass. "You better keep the pussy outside while we at work—the stuff we spray don't smell like roses." He flashed her that wild beaming grin. "We be through in a hour or less, ma'am."

With the helpless rueful look I recalled from when I'd shown her the cut cable wire, she stood aside and let us troop into the house behind our leader and, like any normal housewife suddenly besieged by contractors, tried simultaneously to keep an eye on us and stay out of our way. Thus the carnival began. The six of us spread out over that house with our spray cans and hoses and squirted liquid insecticide along every inch of baseboard. We opened every closet door, every cupboard and cabinet, shining flashlight beams into the crevices, tapping the walls, probing the stairs, pulling out all the stops to appear a fighting legion whose mission was to make this place hell on earth for cockroach Americanus.

Behind the facade of our assault, I searched the house. Only in the most superficial way, of course, since Mrs. Young might have been observing me at any moment, but it was a beginning and would save me time and energy later on. Three of the four upstairs bedrooms and one of the baths were clean but bare. They might hold crannies where a roach could hide, but not a sheaf of love ditties. Mrs. Young understandably enough was a few feet behind me as I sprayed the one furnished bedroom, in whose intimate corners any number of poems from Charles Kilby might be concealed. The living room, dining room, breakfast nook, kitchen, odds-and-ends room cluttered with stuff that a respectable Goodwill store would have junked, any one of them might have been the place, and the organized chaos of the bug crusade gave me no chance to explore them in detail. I was going to have a busy night.

The basement to which Landy and I and three of the others separately descended was huge and damp-smelling and crammed with junk that probably had lain there for generations. We spent twenty minutes in the bowels of the house, spraying, tapping beams, poking in dark corners, futzing around till enough time had passed so that Mrs. Young, if she had noticed, would have forgotten exactly how many workmen had gone down there. When the backs of the three munchkins were turned I gave a tug at Landy's arm, and the next minute he began herding the trio at calculated intervals up the rickety wooden stairs to the main floor. He and I were alone in the basement then. He shook my hand good luck and yanked on the light cord and trudged topside in the wake of his cohorts, leaving me in the dark.

I shuddered. I almost followed him up those stairs into the light. What restrained me was neither courage nor sense of duty but pure dumb stubbornness. I had spent huge sums of Omnitron's money and gone through several identities and all sorts of contortions just to secrete myself in this house, and I was not about to cut and run at this stage of the operation. Behold the dear old Vietnam mentality, the noble Nicaragua syndrome! *Milo,* my voice told me, *you belong in the Pentagon. You think like one of them.*

I tucked under my arm the green metal box I'd lugged through the charade alongside my genuine spraying gear, tiptoed across the dank basement to a heavy wooden door at the far end. The door was unstuck now, but when we'd first come down it had taken Landy and me together to tug it open so we could zap whatever was behind that barrier with insecticide. What was behind it was a cubicle the size of a large closet, lined with rusted steel shelving that was now empty but had once, if my nose was any judge, held cans of paint. The darkness in that hole was absolute. There was an electric-bulb socket in the wall but no bulb, and I hadn't thought to pack one in my kit. The only way of letting air into the cubicle was to keep the entrance door ajar, which didn't help much. All in all, the place made a cell in the Lubyanka look good by comparison. I thanked heaven for it and let myself in and listened to the clatter of feet and the muffled voices and the tapping and the hiss of liquid death into crevices. After a while the noises died away. I heard slammed doors, footsteps receding, and very faintly, from the street, the clash of gears as the van pulled away. Not a single sound was unexpected. As far as I could tell by ear alone, Mrs. Young had not an inkling that one of the invading Killabuggers was still her guest.

I pressed the readout button on my watch. 5:24. The TV game shows had given way to the local news, but there in my chilly little den I had just begun to play a game of my own, in which I was the sole contestant. The name of the game was Settle Down and Wait. With a warm shirt and slacks beneath my coveralls and thermal undies next to the skin, cold wouldn't faze me. With sandwiches and a thermos of hot spiced glühwein in my green metal lunch box, neither would hunger. As long as the lady upstairs stayed at home and awake I had nowhere to go and nothing to do. Except think.

She seemed to be the real Constance Young. She claimed to have the turgid lyrics written to her by a love-smitten Kilby when both of them had been in their teens. She wasn't keeping those poetic gems in a safe-deposit box because, at least here in Monckton, she had no such box. She had installed a state-of-the-art burglar alarm system in this rented house at her own expense. She visited no one and had no visitors, which suggested that at least in Monckton there wasn't a soul to whom she would have entrusted the verses. Even though every line of reasoning wavers, even though there was always the possibility that they were somewhere else, say in an out-of-town deposit box or with a friend in Lamoni, Iowa, my instincts told me she'd keep them close at hand. There was also the possibility that she didn't have them any more, that she'd made a better deal with the Drakean Union, turned the stuff over to Rathjen and his lawyers. But then why would she be staying on here, living like a nun in this nothing city? All the inner voices on which I depend for advice were screaming at me that I'd been right all along. The poems were somewhere in this house.

All through the sounds of early evening, the cat mewing for din-din and the whirr of the electric can opener and the clink of knife and fork on plate and the gurgle of the dishwasher and the muffled voices first of TV news readers and then of the sitcom stars, I sat in the dark and went over the chain of instinct and reasoning that had brought me here. Every link held up.

The process wasn't continuous. I would eat half a sandwich, warm the inner man with a slug of glühwein, and every so often I would be assailed by the impulse to rocket madly out of the basement as I fantasized a roach army crawling across my body.

As the evening wore down and the sounds of action-detective shows and sitcoms and finally the late news percolated into my hidey-hole, I turned my thoughts elsewhere. To be precise, on my strange black sidekick, Dave Landy. I couldn't make head nor tails of the man. In Nam he'd been a grunt, and by his own admission a war criminal and druggie. Back in the States he'd been a street hustler and thief, apparently preying for the most part on other blacks. He hated those past selves now and credited McGaughy with having straightened him out. How had those two met? What magic had that wizened sorcerer worked? Was it like the spell he'd woven around Kilby? Landy's infatuation with La Verne De Nise Nixon-Markson was painfully obvious. Why did he choose not to go beyond looking googly-eyed at her whenever he thought no one was watching him? Well, that much at least I could figure. She had a J.D. after her name and a responsible position, he had no education and a checkered past. And hadn't he said something about his manhood having been left behind in Nam? Suddenly I knew that hadn't been a metaphor. Besides, the woman's name was hyphenated, which, if I remembered feminist nomenclature correctly, meant that she was married. Had McGaughy taught him the married ones were out of bounds? McGaughy, Kilby, Landy. A threesome, a trinity. I wasn't sure I'd ever understand them.

At 11:05 P.M. by the luminous readout on my wrist, the distant TV sounds died and I heard the hollow gurgle of water through pipes. Mrs. Young was preparing for bed. I took my mind off my discomfort by imagining her in the shower.

How long before she'd fall into deep sleep was anyone's guess. I played it safe and gave her ninety minutes. Sat there shivering on the concrete, hearing or thinking I heard tiny skittery noises in the walls. Counting minutes that dragged like weeks.

The instant my readout flashed 12:35 I roused myself. Tiptoed across the basement and up the creaky steps with my work shoes under one arm and the lunch box with the empty thermos and my long ago discarded mustache under the other. The door at the stairhead was locked but didn't stay that way. The Housebreaker's Friend, a special wire loop which I am never without, took care of that. I shut the door gingerly behind me but didn't lock it again, knowing I'd have to spend more time in that dismal paint room if tonight's exploration didn't pan out. I stretched my cramped muscles and yawned and, with ears cocked for danger sounds, slipped down the front hall into the living room, which was as good a place as any to begin.

Searching an occupied house, in total silence and with no light except the glimmers from the street and an occasional stab from a pencil flashlight, ranks among my least favorite ways to spend the night. I pawed through credenza drawers, hefted chair and sofa cushions, lifted the rug, leafed through shelves of book-club novels. I took down each painting from the wall and felt its backside for a bulge. Nothing. I tackled the dining room. Ran my hands across the underside of the table and breakfront and buffet, opened silver chests, did whatever could be done without noise. Nothing. Breakfast nook likewise. The kitchen would have to wait till Mrs. Young left the house on her next shopping errand; too much risk of a pot or pan clattering.

I was finishing the breakfast nook when my ears caught a hard rhythmic pattering sound. Rain drumming on pavement. I froze. Would she hear it, get up to shut the windows or let in the cat? No. On this floor all the windows were already down, and the cat hadn't been out in the yard last night when I'd cut the cable wire, so why would he be out tonight? I stayed frozen for five minutes, then relaxed and pressed my readout button. 2:52. More than two hours wasted. I was about ready to scuttle back to the basement and try to grab a few hours' sleep, but I decided to do the closets first.

There were two, one at each end of the front hall. The coat closet at right angles to the entrance door was easy. At the hall's far end, between the archway into the living room and the door to the kitchen, was the other hall closet, my next and final stop this session.

I had checked it briefly while performing my Rambo act among the roaches. The upper half was shelved and held the usual assortment of accumulated junk: folded grocery bags, light bulbs, plastic freezer containers, a couple of quart jugs. The lower half was unshelved and held a tall stack of newspapers, which I had dragged into the hall so I could spray the baseboards behind them. Mrs. Young had been standing behind me at the time, and I'd had no chance to inspect the closet further, but as I stood in front of it now in the dark I remembered that for a split second yesterday afternoon, something in or about that place had touched a nerve. Whatever it was eluded me now, but maybe, I thought, another look would bring the memory back.

So I assumed the lotus position in front of the open

closet door and eyeballed the tower of newspapers. Three feet high, neat as a marine's footlocker—well, I had already known she was a neatsy lady, that wasn't what had bothered me. I slipped the topmost paper from the stack, set it in my lap, trained the spot of light from my flash on the masthead. It was the Monckton *Conservator* for March 8, 1985, more than eight months ago.

I reached for the next. Monckton *Conservator* for March 9. I reached in and pulled out the uppermost half of the stack and reached in again and fished out the lower half and focused the flashbeam on the dateline of the issue at the bottom of the heap. May 25. Almost six months old. And I had found no pile of more recent numbers of the paper anywhere in my search. Why would she systematically dump the issues from May 26 to the present and keep the ones from March 9 to late May in a meticulous stack? Why would she have arranged the stack she did keep with the earliest date topmost and the most recent at the bottom, instead of in reverse chronological order as normal people would, putting each day's discarded paper at the top so she wouldn't have to tug and lift the pile as it grew heftier? Now I knew what had touched that nerve.

Where does the wise man hide a tree? In the forest. Where does the wise woman hide a small pile of papers? In a large pile of papers.

They're here, one of my voices told me.

I picked up the *Conservator* for March 7 and, with infinite care, shook it out. Nothing was inside that shouldn't have been.

I did the same with the issues for March 8, 9, and 10. Zilch.

Then I put my brain in gear.

If the Kilby poems were hidden in this stack, she must have had a reason for arranging the stack as she had, the troublesome way, earliest date topmost. What could that reason be? Well, if the poems were thrust inside one of the *Conservators,* she'd need to remember the date of the issue she'd used, and she'd probably want it to be relatively close to the top of the stack for easy access. Within the time period represented by that stack, which was the earliest date that anyone could easily remember? March 17. St. Patrick's Day. I groped for that issue with hands trembling in anticipation and shook it out.

A sheaf of handwritten pages torn from a cheap spiral-bound student notebook sailed out of the innards of the sports section and into my waiting lap.

It was all I could do to stifle the yip of joy I wanted to let loose.

I trained the beam on the topmost page of the sheaf. In that roving dot of light the handwriting struck my inexpert eye as all too similar to the penmanship on the holographic will that Charles Brockden Kilby might or might not have scrawled in the last moments of his life. As for the content of the verse, it was as awful as I had expected. One sample quatrain should more than suffice:

> My sweet, you once inspirited
> My poor poetic pen
> But now it wends its weary way alone
> Like Robin Hood without his merry men.

I flipped at breakneck pace through the sheets of lined notebook paper, scanning each ditty for a fraction of a second, my eye alert for one particular ode that I had seen before. A third of the way through the sheaf, I found it.

> My dear, no mouse will ever chew
> Our sacred cheese of love
> Nor will I e'er see buzzard wings
> Upon my turtledove.

There it sat in my fevered palm, the one and only ninety million dollar mouse. I thought I heard one of my voices whispering something about it in my ear.

Before I could focus on it a yowl split my eardrums and my rear end leapt three inches off the floor, the flash clattering out of my fingers onto the hardwood. Halfway down the hall, eyes glowing at me in the dimness, was Jim Socks. Just what the damn situation needed. First the mouse, now the cat.

Which padded over to me on silent paws and went down on the floor and rolled over on his back and offered himself to be rubbed and scratched. Half of me wanted to strangle the beast. He yowled again. I reached out with my one hand and rubbed his belly and under his chin just as I had in my TV repairman incarnation yesterday, while with the other hand I tried to clean up the mess of papers I'd made. The cat started purring blissfully. The sound seduced me. Rearranging newspapers in their original order on the closet floor, and at the same time gently ministering to Jim Socks's forehead and ears, consumed all of my attention. I let my guard down. Stopped listening for the telltale noises for which I should have stayed alert.

So that when the hall light snapped on and she stood there in robe and soft slippers with her hair falling loose around her shoulders and a Colt .38 Woodsman in her hand trained at the top of my head, I was not only dazzled by the brightness and surprised by the swiftness of her approach. My heart stopped. I sat rooted to the hardwood as if the Woodsman were a paralyzer ray in a cheap sci-fi movie.

"Let go of my cat!" she commanded in a voice cold with fury.

That unfroze me. I released Jim Socks and doubled up on the floor, convulsed by a fit of the giggles, while the cat rolled to its feet and stalked haughtily out of the hall and into the kitchen, where sat the bowl of milk that no doubt had been its destination before it encountered me.

Now that she saw me full face and in decent light, it didn't take her long to remember where she'd seen me before, especially since my Killabugger mustache was nesting in the bottom of my lunch box. I saw the spark of recognition come alive in her eyes and knew she understood exactly how I'd slipped through her defenses. I thought I saw her finger tensing on the trigger. Mother of Mercy, was this the end for Milo? Riddled with bullets by an outraged woman for letting loose a few roaches in her house?

Long ago I had sworn never to go gently into that good night from whose bourne no traveler returns. "May I explain?" I asked desperately. "Just for two minutes?" Which was the underestimate of the century since even for the world's champion motormouth the telling of the story would have taken at least an hour. But I did not perceive myself to be in a strong bargaining position at the moment.

"Put your hands up while you're talking," she said. "You might have a gun in your clothes."

"Mrs. Young," I said politely, "I'm very tired, I've been up all night, I don't have a gun, I mean you no harm, I'm sitting here helpless. Do I *have* to keep my hands up while I talk?"

She took some time to think. To me it seemed like several hours but objectively no more than fifteen seconds could have passed before she spoke again.

"You can keep your hands down," she said. "But sit on them."

Obediently I tucked my paws under my butt and tried not to show the wave of relief that flooded me. The psychological dynamics of these gunpoint situations have always intrigued me. I knew now that the woman didn't have the killer instinct. Having conceded me this small favor, she wouldn't shoot me. At least not if I didn't provoke her.

"You were going to explain something," she reminded me.

"I was," I said, feeling my way with infinite caution like a young soldier in the middle of a minefield. "But then I realized you'll never believe me."

"Try," she said, and this time I was certain her finger tightened on the trigger.

"My name is Lattman," I began hastily. "I'm a private investigator."

"Let's see you prove that," she interrupted.

"I don't carry genuine ID when I'm pretending to be somebody else. But if you'd care to drive me to the Airhotel when I've finished, I've got identification there."

"We'll see," she said. "Keep talking."

"I was hired by Omnitron Technologies after you sent Colonel Shaw the letter asking for $2,000,000 for the Kilby poems and your testimony. Shaw wanted my opinion on whether the poems were genuine. That meant I had to get a look at the originals."

"You mean to steal them," she corrected me acidly.

"Well," I admitted, "maybe borrow them for a little while. But couldn't you try to see it from the company's perspective for a minute? Let's assume the poems are genuine. Even if I'd stolen them for keeps, it wouldn't help Omnitron much. If the handwriting matched up with Kilby's holographic will, you could still testify for the Drakean Union and prove your story with photocopies. You must have made a few sets for safety's sake. And if the handwriting on the poems didn't match the will, Omnitron would need your testimony to prove the authenticity of the originals. Let me put it another way. If those poems are genuine, they're not going to help either side much without your cooperation."

"And if they're not genuine?" she said.

I dimly recalled Shaw's remark on that subject during the gourmet dinner and, finding its philosophy sound, tried to parrot it. "In that case," I said, "the company would love you to make a deal with the other side. When you get on the stand, Omnitron's lawyers will . . . " I was going to say "rip you to shreds" but, considering that she still held a gun on me, discreetly let the sentence trail off instead.

She knew what I meant, though, and thought about it so long and so hard I could almost hear the gears grinding in her head. Then unaccountably she jumped from that topic to another. "How do I know you're not working for Rathjen?" she said.

For the first time I felt hate in the house with us. It was the way her voice changed, the way she altered her body language, shouted at me that if she thought I was a minion of the high ferio she would gleefully empty the pistol in my face. I scrambled for an answer that would keep her from squeezing the trigger, and the hell of it was that, sitting on the floor with my hands stuck under my ass, there was no way I could convince her. I might have described the contents of the letter she'd sent to Shaw, or have offered to show her a copy if she'd take me to the Airhotel where I'd kept the file, but she could argue that a Drakean spy in Omnitron headquarters had leaked a copy of the letter to the Union, and how could I refute that?

I couldn't figure out what to say to the furious woman until all of a sudden I realized that her fury was telling me something, and that in turn explained a little puzzle that, ever since I'd fallen into this morass, had gnawed at me.

"Oho," I said softly, and looked up at her with not a scintilla of fear in my eyes. "So *that's* why you wrote the letter that way!"

"What are you talking about?" she demanded.

"Your letter to Shaw," I said. "You were so emphatic that you were making your offer just to him, not to the other side."

"So what?"

"Economics teaches us," I replied smugly, "that ordinarily people act to maximize their take. The way to maximize your take would have been to let both sides know what you had and get them bidding against each other. You didn't do that. You must have had a reason for not doing it. You've just told me the reason. Now if you wouldn't mind explaining *why* you hate Rathjen so much—"

"Why should I explain anything to a burglar?" she broke in coldly.

"Because I hate the fucker too," I said. And then the floodgates opened, and without mentioning names or places I told her the story Sarah Rogers had told me that night in my suite at the Beverly. Perhaps in one respect I shaded the truth a bit, made it seem that Sarah and I were more than just casual acquaintances, but otherwise I told it straight. As I talked I watched Mrs. Young's face turn grim with rage again, but this time not at me. When I finished, she was dead calm. She put the Woodsman in the pocket of her robe and came toward me, holding out her hands to help me to my feet.

"I believe you," she said, and then shouted it. "My God, I believe you! Oh, God, God, there's someone on my side at last!" And mirabile dictu, she fell against me in that unmistakable way that meant she wanted me to hold her, and I put my arms around her and hugged her and felt the salt of her tears against my cheek and wondered if I'd fallen down the rabbit hole.

Fifteen minutes later we were side by side on the chesterfield in the living room, with mugs of coffee laced with brandy on the table before us and one shaded lamp burning low. The rain still drummed against the windows and the street but it was a friendly drumming now, something to help the flowers grow. With Jim Socks sprawled contentedly on the rug between our feet, Constance Williams Young told me her story. We were still talking when the sun rose.

"I spent my first seventeen years in this city," she began. "I hated it. Monckton had all the shabbiness and despair of a dying steeltown and all the self-righteousness of a fundamentalist revival camp."

"Still does," I said.

"I was a sixties kid, a rebel. I didn't know what I wanted but I knew it wasn't here. I stayed long enough to graduate from high school and three weeks later I was on the road, hitchhiking west."

"You left your parents?"

"I left two people who were sorry excuses for parents. They're dead now," she said. "Anyway, I bummed around northern California for a few years, making a living as best I could, cocktail waitress, go-go dancer. Once in a while I'd let a guy I slept with give me a little money. And then . . . well, I met this man."

The way her voice went soft and dreamy told me that, whoever he was, for her he was the only one.

"His name was Jon Young. He was a realtor from a small town in Iowa, in San Francisco for a convention. He was twenty years older than me, his wife and son had been killed in an auto accident a couple of years before, and he was very lonely. I was waitressing in the revolving bar on the top floor of the convention hotel. He came in and found an empty table on the carousel and kept ordering bourbons on the rocks every ten or fifteen minutes and kept looking out the windows at nothing. It was a very foggy night. I think it was his fourth drink I was serving him when he asked me my name and told me his and said he'd turned forty that day and no one had wished him a happy birthday."

"And you said happy birthday to him," I said.

"It was a slow night," she said. "We talked awhile, I didn't have any other customers to serve and he looked like he'd be good for a nice tip if I treated him decently. He asked me if I'd like to go somewhere with him for a bite to eat when the bar closed, and I guess I was lonely too and, you know, one thing led to another, and I went down to his room with him." She chuckled softly with remembered pleasure. "Neither of us got a thing to eat till morning, and he never went to another session of that convention. We got to know each other better in the next three days than most people can do in three years. He asked me to marry him and come back to Lamoni, Iowa as his wife, and I said yes."

"You don't need to tell me it worked out beautifully," I said.

Her eyes glowed with the special radiance that nothing can bring to a woman's face except Mr. Right.

"We had five great years. I went to secretarial school, and he put me to work in his office, and I became his assistant. I did most of the business correspondence, even with lawyers, and I'd never even gone to college."

So that explains the legalisms in her letter to Colonel Shaw, I thought. One more little puzzle untangled.

"And then one day in the early spring of 1976 everything started to fall apart," she said. "I can still tell you the exact date, it was April 4. Jon was in Kansas City on business for a week, and I was running the office single-handed, and just as I was closing up for the evening this young man in a very expensive three-piece suit walked in and said he'd like to talk to me and showed me his card. It was a strange business card. Didn't give an address or a phone number but just his name and 'Attorney at Law.' "

"What name?"

"You may have heard of him," she said. "He's become pretty important in Drakean circles recently. Mark Dextraze."

I almost leapt off the chesterfield in my excitement. "Dextraze? The soprano that gives all those sermons on the Drakean radio station? The one who's next in line to take over as boss of the Union?"

She nodded slowly, all the radiance gone from her now. "He's aged some in ten years, but that's who it was. I'll never forget that cold dead face. When I think of the two of us alone in Jon's office that evening, I feel as if there's a block of stone in my throat."

"He attacked you? Did something to you sexually?" I remembered what his boss had done to Sarah Rogers in New York, and my skin crawled.

"He never laid a finger on me. No, this all started out as an ordinary conversation, not even about business. He said he knew Chuck Kilby slightly and wondered if I'd kept up with him at all since we were at Monckton High, and I said I hadn't. He told me that Chuck had gone into the high-tech field and was a multimillionaire already, and I said I was glad to hear it. Chuck had been sort of a science nerd in school, an okay kid but brilliant and painfully shy and withdrawn and friendless. He'd had a, well, a lonely adolescent's crush on me for a few months, and I'd tried to be nice to him, and he'd written, oh, fifty or sixty absolutely dreadful love poems and slipped them into my schoolbooks or my locker when I wasn't looking. And Dextraze was telling me about how successful Chuck was, and I was thinking that wasn't it nice of Chuck to ask this friend of his who was passing through to stop off and say hello to me for him, and all of a sudden the conversation went crazy."

"What happened?"

"Dextraze told me that he represented Dr. Rathjen, the high ferio of the Drakean Union. I knew about the Union, of course, from the years I'd lived in Monckton, and Dextraze knew I knew. Suddenly I caught on that he knew an awful lot about me. He said he had a business proposition he wanted me to consider. I told him when Jon would be back in the office, and he said the proposition wasn't for Jon, it was just for me." She fought back a shudder, reached for the laced coffee to warm herself. "He offered me half a million dollars cash if I would divorce Jon, go back with him to California, where Chuck lived most of the time, insinuate myself into Chuck's life again, and seduce him and get him to marry me. The way I'd done with Jon, he said. Dextraze promised to give me all the backing I needed for as long as it took to drag Chuck to the altar. He said the Union could falsify pregnancy tests on me, or one of its people whose blood type was the same as Chuck's could make me pregnant, and we could force him into marrying me that way and get me an abortion later. Mr. Lattman, that man sat there in my husband's office and laid out this insane scheme as if it were a blueprint for a building! After a year or so of marriage to Chuck I was supposed to dump him and go to the lawyers Dextraze picked out for me, and they would file for divorce and take Chuck to the cleaners. Under the community property laws I'd wind up owning half the stock in Chuck's company. Dextraze said I could keep ten percent of my share as a bonus, and the rest I was to sign over to the Drakean Union."

I had heard of outrageous plots before, and in all modesty I admit I had perpetrated a few wild ones myself, but for sheer lunatic chutzpah this Dextraze Special left my feeble efforts toiling in the rear. I kept my thoughts buttoned up and nodded to her to go on.

"He saw that I wasn't looking interested, I guess, so then he said if I wanted to make a lot more money out of it for myself, he had an alternative to propose. After I married Chuck I was to see to it that he made a will leaving me *all* his stock in the company. Then after what Dextraze called a decent interval, the Union would have someone—have some of its people kill Chuck and make it look like an accident or something. They'd make sure, of course, that I'd have a perfect alibi for when it happened. Then after I came into Chuck's estate I could keep a third and give the rest to the Union."

I thought of Mrs. Young, still in her twenties, sitting in that Iowa real estate office in the heartland twilight and having to listen to that smooth-tongued sack of shit, and for the life of me I couldn't decide what I would have done if I'd been in her shoes, so I asked her the inevitable question. "What did you do?"

"I told him to get out," she said, "or I'd call the police."

With great difficulty I resisted the impulse to applaud. "Did he go?"

"Oh yes, he left peacefully. But before he did, he gave me a warning. He said that if I didn't want to work with him, well, that was my choice. But if I ever told the police about his visit, first of all he could produce a dozen witnesses to prove he'd been a thousand miles away from Iowa tonight, so no one would believe me. And he said there was a cell of secret Drakeans in the state troopers, and if I went to the police about him, I'd be kidnapped by those troopers and gang-raped and mutilated. Even if I just told Jon about the visit, he said the same thing would happen to me, and they'd cripple Jon too. Then he took back his business card from me and gave me a polite little European bow and walked out of there as if he were king of the world. I heard his car driving off toward the interstate a minute later."

"What did you do?"

"I sat there shaking like a leaf! I'd never gone through anything like that before."

"You never told the cops or your husband?"

"I was terrified. I guess I did what many women do when they've been raped. Tried to convince myself it was a bad dream, tried to get on with my life. Then"—I saw the corners of her mouth tremble—"something even worse happened. A few months later Jon went to the doctor for a routine checkup and was told he had inoperable liver cancer. He died that same month. We only had two weeks to say good-bye." The tears flowed freely then, and I reached for her and held her gently until she was in control again.

"Two weeks after I buried him, I went away. I had to be by myself for a while and think about the future. I was staying in Boston for a few days, and then one evening I was walking along Massachusetts Avenue, just window shopping, and a man bumped into me from behind and said, 'Pardon me,' and it was Dextraze again! And before I could say anything, he looked straight at me and said, 'Now that we've taken care of your husband for you, would you care to reconsider our offer?' "

"What did you do?"

"I am not Superwoman. I fell apart. My mouth started flapping without saying anything, and my legs crumpled and I collapsed on the sidewalk. A crowd collected around me, a policeman came and an ambulance came, and they took me to the emergency room and kept me overnight for observation."

"And you never told anyone about Dextraze stopping you on the street?"

"That time," she said, "I did tell someone. As soon as I left the hospital I went to the police station near my hotel and talked to a detective sergeant, a young man, his name was Patrick Ryan. He heard me out, and then he said there was no way I could ever prove any of it, and if the Drakean Union ever heard of my charges they'd sue me for millions of dollars for slander and drag me through the courts for years, the way they do whenever anyone dares to say anything about them they don't like."

"Was this Ryan a Drakean?"

"He said he was a Catholic, but his commander was a Drakean. He promised not to make a report on our conversation, and that way his boss wouldn't see it and I wouldn't get in trouble with the Union. Mr. Lattman, I walked out of that police station knowing my husband had been murdered, knowing the Drakeans had given him cancer somehow, or poisoned him so it looked like cancer, just to get rid of him so they could offer me a second chance to marry Chuck Kilby for them, and I couldn't prove it, I couldn't get anyone to help me, I couldn't even talk about it! That was how I lived for the next several years. Terror, outrage, frustration. Two or three times I came close to checking myself into a mental hospital. But the years went by and—and nothing happened. And I suppose, well, I adjusted to the situation, got used to it the way eventually you can get used to anything, even living in Auschwitz. I didn't hurt them and they didn't hurt me."

"What broke the stalemate?"

"When I read last year that Chuck died," she said, "and that he'd written that will leaving everything to the Union in the minute before his death. I knew they'd finally gotten to him some other way than through me. They'd tortured him or hypnotized him and made him write that will, and then they injected him with something that made it look like he'd died of a heart attack."

"You're giving them credit for supernatural powers," I told her, quietly so as not to start a debate with her. "The Drakeans are a pack of thugs and killers and they have clout in some high places, but they are not gods. Look, the best forensic pathologists in the country examined

Kilby's body. They found no signs of foul play. Understand? None. He had a history of heart attacks, and he died of a heart attack."

"Pathologists can be bribed or terrorized too," she said. "Or they could be Drakeans themselves."

"Like the doctor your husband went to in Iowa who found the liver cancer?"

"Yes!" Her shout galvanized the cat, who leapt off the chesterfield and padded out of the room. "Maybe," she said.

Much as I'd longed to hurt Rathjen and Dextraze and their disciples before, now I wanted it worse. I wanted to squash them as I'd squashed the roaches in this house for the way they'd made this sweet woman beside me into a quivering paranoid. I reached for her again, took her hands between my own.

"I understand," I said. "I won't argue with you. Okay, so when Kilby died you decided to come back into the picture, right?"

"Does it sound crazy to you?"

"A little," I admitted. "They kill your husband and you don't fight back, they ruin your life and you don't fight back, they kill a high-school classmate who meant almost nothing to you and you fight."

"I know," she said. "But I don't have much else to do with my life, and Jon's business left me enough to live on for a few years, and I'm stronger now than I was. And if they've done all this to me, they've done it to God knows how many other women. Their religion depends on abuse and terror."

"All religions do," I said.

"This one will not get away with it anymore," she said. "All I live for now is to rip it apart."

"And those love poems from Kilby years ago are your weapon?"

"Yes. That's why I came back to Monckton, and

rented this house, and wrote Colonel Shaw that letter. I didn't want two million dollars from the company, I wanted the letter to leak to Rathjen and Dextraze, I wanted them to come to me and make me a better offer for the poems and my testimony. If I approached them, especially after what happened years ago, they'd be bound to suspect I was up to something, but not if they approached me."

"But the hell of it is," I said, "that they haven't approached you. Right?"

She chewed her lower lip with the fury of a low-level employee pounding the heavy bag at the fitness center after a grinding day. "I can't understand it! I've been waiting so many months and nothing's happened!"

Shaw's security mania made the silence from the Drakean camp quite easy to understand, but I took another and gentler line with her. "You see?" I said. "They're not everywhere, and they're not omnipotent. But suppose they did contact you, or let's say they do it tomorrow, or next week. What would you do then?"

"Join them," she said. "Mr. Lattman, the really technical part of the will contest is over now, it's settled that California law controls Chuck's estate. From now on the case is going to be a media circus, a duel of wills with billions of dollars at stake. Eventually I'm going to be called as a witness. I'm going to be on the stand with dozens of reporters in the courtroom and all the network TV cameras running. And that's when I drop my little bombshell on the Drakean Union."

Hoo God, I thought. That videocassette of *And Justice for All* on the stack under her TV! She watches Al Pacino stand up in court and tell the jury in a voice choked with rage that his client is a sociopath and a pervert and guilty as hell, and she thinks she can pull more or less the same stunt in a courtroom out in the real world. How could I get the message through to her that her grandiose scheme was just as cockeyed and unworkable as the Dextraze Special that had made her devote her life to retaliation?

"I don't think," I ventured, "that a judge is going to let you bad-mouth the Union in open court for as long as you feel like."

"He will," she said, "when I start by telling him the truth about the poems from Chuck."

I didn't say anything. An I-Know-Something-You-Don't-Know confidence had crept into her voice, and I sensed she was poised to share her secret with me, so I sat back against the corner of the chesterfield and counted to myself and waited for her to spit it out.

"They're fakes," she said.

Somehow it didn't surprise me. Sitting on the floor in front of her closet, skimming through the sheaf of poems for a minute or two before I was interrupted by the cat, I had heard one of my voices whispering to me. This usually means that my instincts have caught something my brain has missed. Now I knew what it was. Before she had a chance to fill in the details I rose, stretched, excused myself, and went back to the closet and pulled out the issue of the *Conservator* in which the poems were sandwiched and brought the sheaf into the living room, where I pawed through the immortal verses for the second time that night. Which one had triggered the alarm bell in my head? Not the one about Robin Hood and the poor poetic pen. Not thet one that began "A lovely girl this day for me/Is sitting under the cherry tree." Could it have been the mouse epic? I reread that marvelous opening stanza in the cone of light from the table lamp.

> My dear, no mouse will ever chew
> Our sacred cheese of love
> Nor will I . . .

That was it. This time my voice screamed at me, a gong went off in my head, and bleary-eyed as I was, I saw it.

The word will in line one looked too much like the word will in line three.

No matter how often you write the same word or set of words, even if you write them a few seconds apart, they never look identical. Show me two stroke-for-stroke identical signatures and I'll show you a forgery. The only way that can happen is if one is traced from the other. I couldn't be certain the two "will" words were identical without taking a photocopy of the verse and holding the line one will and the line three will against each other, but even to the naked eye, or at least to my naked eye, they looked too much alike to be real. If I'd been astute enough to run that test on the photocopy Mrs. Young had sent Shaw, I wouldn't have needed to come to Monckton at all. A humbling thought.

While I was thinking, the lady of the plot was filling in the details.

"Chuck had given me real poems very much like those when we were in school here," she said. "But I threw them away as junk a long time ago. My God, they were awful! Why would I have wanted to keep them? I didn't know Chuck was going to become rich and famous."

I put down the sheaf of verse on the coffee table and picked up my end of the dialogue. "So years later, after Kilby died and you dreamed up your scheme, you sort of had to get the poems written all over again?"

"That's right."

"Which means you had to find a good document forger."

"I was lucky," she said. "Back when I was bumming around California I'd met a few people who were, well, connected. One of them owed me a favor. I found him again and asked him to introduce me to someone who could forge me some papers. I had to sort of make up the texts, I couldn't remember exactly how the real poems went, so I made them as dumb as I could. And I had a few genuine samples of Chuck's handwriting, an autograph in my yearbook, one or two old Christmas cards I'd never thrown away."

"And you wanted someone to forge a couple dozen poems with just that to work from? There aren't five guys in the country—"

"And I found one of them," she broke in. "In San Francisco. Oh, God, what was that little man's name, Winkle, Dinkle?"

"Try Hackel," I said. "Skinny old guy, false teeth, no chin, works out of a photomart on Geary Street? Humpty Hackel." I forebore to mention that once or twice I had used the man's prodigious talents myself. But never again. Time and age had clearly begun to take their toll on him. Instead of doing the job right, starting from scratch on the word "will" in line three, he'd cheated and traced the word from where it appeared in line one. I wondered how often he'd cut the same corner elsewhere in the poetic sheaf. But none of this was Mrs. Young's business, so I veered the conversation onto another subject. "I'll bet he charged you for a job like that."

"Those poems cost half what Jon left me in his will," she said. "I don't mind, if they take me where I want to go." She gave me an indrawn calculating look of the sort that evil women used to give weak-willed men in the Films Noir of the 1940s. "Mr. Lattman, you obviously know your way around. Can you see to it that the Union finds out I have these, and then let me take it from there?"

"Maybe," I said, "but I won't."

"Why not?" she demanded, more than a little angrily. "You say you hate them too."

"That is not the issue." My exasperation was beyond stifling, and I resisted with difficulty the urge to throttle sense into her. "Lady, you are going about your vendetta like a lunatic. You want to trick Rathjen into putting you on the witness stand, giving you a forum where you can dump on the Union in front of all the media. Do you have a death wish or something? Look what they did to the woman I told you about, and she had a national newsmagazine behind her and was trying to write a *balanced* story!"

"Mr. Lattman." Her voice was too quiet. It reminded me of a field just before the funnel cloud touches down. "You still don't understand. I want them to have no choice but to kill me. In public, while I'm exposing them, with the whole country watching. I've spent most of my money and almost a year of my life trying to make them do that. I don't care what happens to me if I can take them with me." A pulse twitched at the base of her throat. "If you agree to help me, I'll make out a will, you'll get everything after they kill me. If you don't—I'll connect with Rathjen somehow and keep working on my own." The coiled-spring tightness seemed to flow out of her body. Her head slumped forward as if it were a lead weight. "I'm just so tired of waiting," she said.

In the cold light of self-interest I should have walked away. Omnitron had paid me a magnificent sum to make a judgment about the supposed Kilby poems this woman had offered for sale. I'd earned my money. The rational course would have been to thank her for blowing the scam, catch the first flight back to Jersey, and pick up the second thread of my task—rooting around for the vanished Martin Genetelli. But damn it, the woman was crazy as a bedbug, and it was the Drakean Union poohbahs and their mind games that had pushed her over the edge, and I didn't want her to blow herself up like a Libyan suicide squad fanatic in her frenzy to get even.

Sometimes being rational makes no sense.

"Tell you what," I said. "Now that I know where you

stand, I need some time to figure out the next play. Will you wait a little while longer? Say till a week from today?"

"You can have till tomorrow," she said flatly.

"Three days," I offered. "Take it or leave it."

I could almost see the pros wrestling with the cons inside her sweet mixed-up head. She'd waited so many months already, her scheme to date had been a bust, she'd been playing a lone hand and now a partner had dropped from the sky into her lap. I leaned back on the chesterfield and watched the war of emotions on her face as her nails clawed at the upholstery.

"Three days," she said. Her body seemed to go limp like a deflated balloon, as if she'd expelled something from inside her that had been keeping her strung tight, and her eyes took on a sudden startled look. "My God, it's morning!" she said. "We've been up talking half the night! I haven't done that since Jon died."

"Feel better?"

"I'm exhausted and relieved and—I don't know, I've got this strange feeling that life's just started over for me but I know it really hasn't."

"No surprise," I said. "You were sure you were going to die in your crusade, and now you think maybe you won't have to. What you need right now is a good long nap." I pushed myself off the couch and, once on my feet, swayed groggily for a moment. My workman's clothes felt alive and crawling on me. A long, long, hot shower and a half-day's snooze were at the top of my own priority list at the moment, but at this hour, when all the good burghers of residential Monckton were gulping down their Wheaties—or their apple and orange and hard-boiled egg—and trooping into their Nissans and Hondas for the daily trek to the office, in my frazzled-looking state I had as much chance of hoofing it unobserved from here to Hunter Drive as I had of walking on the Mississippi.

"Stay awhile?" she invited softly.

There were several bedrooms in that house but only one bed, a queen-size with a thick mauve counterpane, rumpled and unmade thanks to the middle-of-the-night disturbance. We slept in the bed together, but I blush to confess we did nothing else there. It was halfway through the afternoon when she drove me downtown and left me off a few blocks from the parking garage where I'd stowed the Camry. Our parting kiss was as chaste as a peck between brother and sister. Damn.

8

When the existence of the Church is threatened, she is released from the commandments of morality. With unity as the end, the use of every means is sanctified, even cunning, treachery, violence, simony, prison, death.

Dietrich von Nieheim, Bishop of Verden,
De Schismate

I TOOK A swim in the Airhotel's heated pool, then a light workout and a run in the health club, then a glass cage back to eighteen-o-eight. Every half hour I put in a fruitless call to Landy's room. He might have been in secret conclave with McGaughy or off on business of his own. Or he might be dead. With animals like Rathjen and Dextraze on the other side, murder was always a possibility. I tried not to think of it. I stood at the window and watched twilight stretching out the shadows like a kid pulling taffy. I tried to think of nothing.

And the result was that I thought of everything.

Once in a rare while the key is placed in our hands. We are sitting in a chair or standing at a window, our minds wandering idly through the infinity of thought, and suddenly we are sucked into the vortex of illumination and whirled around and around and yet we are as still as the silence of the heart of the universe, and we *know*, we grasp the whole of it with the whole of us and it and we are one. In Zen Buddhism the experience is called satori.

It comes unexpected and unbidden but only to those who are prepared. At 5:37 P.M. that Tuesday as I stood at the window of room 1808 in the Airhotel and stared at patterns of shadow, it came to me.

I saw the whole thing.

I heard a sound like nothing human and realized only two or three minutes later that it must have been made by me. By then I was on the bed, sitting upright, scattering over the counterpane the photocopied files I had taken from the meeting at Omnitron. Not in that one, not in that one, there, there it was. The copy of the holographic will Kilby had supposedly written in his last moments. I snatched it off the bed, took it to the coffee table, flicked on the floor lamp, went back to the bed, shuffled through the spare set of photocopies of the forged Kilby love lyrics that Constance Young had given me earlier in the day. *Come on, come on, where are you, goddamn fucking rodent?* So much for my moment of Buddhist contemplation. I was so keyed up that I went through that set three times and missed the one sheet of paper I was scrambling for.

The fourth time through, I found it.

> My dear, no mouse will ever chew
> Our sacred cheese of love
> Nor will I e'er see buzzard wings
> Upon my turtledove.

I held that sheet under the light in one hand and held the copy of the alleged holographic will under the light in the other hand and brought them together in my hands as if in a mating ritual, manipulating the papers under the light until the word will in the will was directly atop the word will in the first line of the poem.

Perfect match. Every stroke of every letter identical.

I manipulated the sheets again until will in the will was

directly atop will in the third line of the poem. Same result.

A maxim from elementary algebra burst up from the pool of memory. Quantities equal to the same quantity are equal to each other.

Whether or not mine is the first satori confirmed by hard evidence virtually on the spot, I leave to the historians of religion. I felt as if the top of my head had blown off. I felt like the lord of creation, I knew so much, I saw so much. *God, God, God,* I kept saying to myself, *it's all there, it's all there!* I catapulted off the bed, started pacing madly about the room, heedless of reality as a whirling dervish, bumping into chairs and tables until the place was a shambles. The room couldn't contain me. I wanted to dance. I wanted to fly. Most of all I wanted to share my sudden insight with someone. Almost anyone. If I didn't translate it into words my insides would burst.

I lurched to the phone on the night table and punched out Landy's room number. It rang and rang and rang and no one picked up. And then I did hear a voice, but it wasn't his, it was one of my own, coming from the cave where my darkest instincts lurk. *He's dead,* the voice told me. *They got him. You're next.* In that instant the balloon of euphoria burst, and I dropped the phone and sat there on the bed, feeling invisible eyes all around the brightly lit room watching me and invisible weapons waiting to tear me, and I shuddered. The anxiety attack lasted a good five minutes. Then I began to think again.

So much had gone right and now things were beginning to go wrong. It was time to close up shop in Monckton, shut down the identities I had activated on this mission, and collect Landy and McGaughy, wherever the hell they were, if they were still alive, and beat a strategic retreat to the East Coast, where I could figure out how to use what I knew in the nice safe cozy environment of midtown Manhattan.

First, however, I had another phone call to make, and prudence dictated that I make it elsewhere than from my room. I shrugged on a sport jacket, slipped out of 1808, took an elevator to the mezzanine level, strolled through randomly chosen corridors to see if I could detect anyone on my tail, then followed the signs to the monorail platform exit and caught a robot car to the airport by the skin of my teeth. No one got in behind me. At the terminal I eased my paranoia by wandering some more, slipping in and out of a gift shop and a cafeteria and a john before I parked myself at a nest of credit-card phones and used the AT & T calling card I maintain in the name of Clayton Cox to make a person-to-person to San Francisco. "The Hackel Photomart on Geary Street," I told the operator. "I want to speak to Mr. Humphrey Hackel." I listened to the clicks and squeals of automated connection, then to the same empty ringing sounds I'd heard from the hotel every time I'd tried to call Landy, but this time not so many rings. They were interrupted by a mechanical lady voice that came on the line with news I was not at all surprised to hear. "We're sorry," the voice said. "The number you have dialed has been disconnected." Pause. "We're sorry," the voice said, "The number you have dialed . . ."

I hung up. Humpty Hackel had run that photomart out of the same cubbyhole office on Geary for a third of a century, and he was much too old to start up in a new location now. Of all my San Francisco contacts, who'd be most likely to know what had happened to the chinless wonder? I thought about it for a minute and settled on Lujan. Dipped into my memory bank of phone numbers, plucked out the one I wanted, and used the Clayton Cox card to place the call, this time station-to-station, to his tavern on Turk Street. A female Hispanic voice came on at the other end.

"Carlos Lujan, por favor," I said.

"Who calls him, please?"

"Señor Delaguerra. Alfonso Delaguerra." It was a name I assumed he would remember since it was he who had stuck it on me six years before during a scam we had pulled that had netted us a quarter mil apiece from a Colombian drug dealer.

"Momentito," she said. I listened to silence for more than a minute before Lujan's low seductive baritone came on the wire.

"So it is Delaguerra again after all this time! Why you be a stranger so much, Delaguerra? You come out here again where the sun is sweet, we drink the margaritas like in the old time, eh?"

"Carlos," I said, "we never drank margaritas or daiquiris or any other south-of-thee-bordair stuff. Your tipple is Irish whisky straight up, Tullamore Dew or Bushmill's."

"Ah," he said. "Bueno. Just wanted to make sure, hermano. What I can do for you?"

"Tell me what's happened to Humpty Hackel. I tried the shop and his phone's disconnected. You know where I can get hold of him?"

"Si," he said. "You come out here and dig him out of the ground, that is how you get hold of him. They find what was left of him two, three months ago. Fished the pieces out of the Russian River."

"Christ," I said softly. "I was afraid it was something like that. You know who did it? Anyone arrested for it yet?"

"I don't think the cops try too hard," Lujan said. "You know how it goes when one of us in the life buys it. Hey, I din' know you and old Humpty was so close, hermano."

"He was like a father to me," I said. "Okay, Carlos, thanks for the poop. See you my next trip West."

Just for the hell of it, I tried one more call before I left the airport. Landy's room still didn't answer.

I boarded another robot car to the Airhotel and escalatored from the monorail platform to the hotel parking lot, where I hunted through the serried ranks of cars and found my Camry and propelled it through the darkness of early evening toward the residential district of Monckton. Every few minutes I checked the rearview mirror for anything resembling a tail, and to make assurance doubly sure I performed some evasive maneuvers through the city streets after exiting the interstate. By the time I turned into the driveway of the safe house and unlocked the garage doors and tucked the Camry within, I was more than half convinced that there was no reason at all to feel alarm. Landy was off somewhere on a toot. McGaughy had never been within a thousand miles of Monckton. Hackel had been hacked up by people who were not now and never had been enforcers for the Drakean Union. None of those enforcers were out to nail me or knew a damn thing about me. In four round trips I loaded into the Camry's trunk everything I had brought to the house: the futon and the spare clothing and faithful Alfred and the leftover chow and wine. I checked once more to make sure I'd forgotten nothing, went through the kitchen door to the garage, unlocked the garage doors from the inside and opened them to the cool dark night.

And to the two men with guns in their mitts who were standing in the doorway.

They moved quietly inside the garage. One of them kept me covered while the other shut the doors and pressed on the overhead light switch and came back and covered me from another angle. They were tall and lanky with salt-and-pepper hair and clefts in their chins and lean waists and pipestem legs. One wore a blue suit with a gray tie and the other a blue suit with a maroon tie. Even in the brightness from the garage ceiling it took me half a minute to recognize them. They were two of the crew Landy had picked up to play bug exterminators at Constance Young's house.

"What the hell do you think you're doing?" I demanded, trying to make myself sound convincingly outraged, though in fact I was quivering with fright, expecting them to blow me away without a word.

"Man wants to see you," Maroon Tie said. His voice was flat and cold like his face. He reached into a side pocket with his left hand and pulled out a filter-tipped cigarette, which he positioned between his sensuous lips, then reached in again and pulled out a Bic and lit the business end. His right hand never moved an inch and his eyes stayed trained on my middle. "Turn," he said. "Spread your arms and legs."

I forced my body to swing around and assume the frisk position with my hands on the Camry's roof. I felt a pair of hands slapping and squeezing me for weapons, smelled tobacco smoke almost under my nose: Maroon Tie. He yanked the wallet from my slacks pocket. "Catch," he grunted, and I heard a slapping sound as it struck the concrete floor. He brought his face around close to mine. "Your fault my brother missed that catch," he said, and touched the glowing end of his cigarette against my earlobe just for a second. I yelped.

"Cut that, Fencl," the second one barked.

Obediently Fencl backed away from me. My ear felt as if it had been held in white-hot pincers.

"Go in the house, Fencl," the second one said. "Bring out a few ice cubes from the fridge, wrapped in a paper towel or something." I heard the scrape of reluctant footsteps as Fencl went off. "You can turn now if you want," number two told me. I pushed myself away from the Camry and stood facing the kindly brother with my hips wedged against the trunk. Fencl came back and handed me a filthy handkerchief stuffed with ice cubes. Without a moment's thought to what germs might be breeding on its surface, I pressed it gratefully against the burning tip of my ear.

Gray Tie meanwhile was pawing deftly through my wallet, pulling out this card and that card, holding them up to the light as if he were myopic. "According to what's in here," he said, "you're at least three different people. You're a guy named Clayton Cox, and you're Peter Porter, and you're also a private snoop by the name of Lattman."

Thinking that his remark didn't call for a reply, I stood mute and nursed my ear.

"Okay, which one is the real you?" he asked.

"You've got the guns," I said. "I'm anyone you want me to be."

"Come *on,* Orvis!" the sadist brother snorted. "Why do we give a shit who he is? Let's take him out and be done with it."

Take him out, take him out. Did that mean that they were going to kill me, or did he mean just take me out of here and bring me someplace else? Fencl had started by saying that a man wanted to see me. That could mean Rathjen or Dextraze, or it could just as well mean Mister Death, only I didn't think Fencl was capable of that sort of sublety. All right, so I was going to be kept alive at least a little while. Whoever wanted to see me obviously wanted to ask me questions. Where would the questioning most likely be done? Either on the campus of Barnabas Drake University or somewhere on Union Island. The improvised ice pack had numbed my ear, but my brain still seemed to be functional, thank heaven.

"Time to go," Orvis murmured, and gestured with his gun for Fencl to unlock the garage doors. "Keep that ice against the burn awhile longer and you won't feel a thing," he assured me. "I want to apologize for what my brother did. No reason for that a-tall."

"Think nothing of it," I said. If I ever got one of those .38s in my hands, I promised myself, I'd leave the two of them with holes where their ears were.

"Now let's all walk out to our car real natural like," Orvis said. "Fencl, you drive, I'll sit in the back with our friend. Clear?" The doors swung back and he motioned me out into the driveway. Fencl pulled the doors shut behind him, and a minute later he came out through the front door and pulled that shut too. The three of us marched down the driveway to the street, where a dark Mercury Lynx hatchback stood at the curb. Hunter Drive stretched placid and empty in both directions. Gold light spilled from house windows and cold white pinpoints of light filled the cloudless night sky. Orvis hustled me into the back seat of the Lynx and piled in beside me while Fencl, with a cigarette still hanging between his lips, slid into the command seat and snapped on the headlights and twisted the ignition key. I knew we'd be heading for the Great River Road and wasted no effort keeping track of our route.

As we rolled through the quiet evening streets, I had another satori.

Two brothers, who looked enough alike to be twins, and did enforcement work for the Drakean Union. Of course! This had to be the pair Sarah Rogers had been visited by, the ones who had come with Rathjen to scar her mind for life. God damn it to hell! Of all the cheap hoodlums that hung out in downtown Monckton, Landy had had to recruit these two creeps whose loyalty was to the other side.

All right, so the damage was done. How much could the other side know? Only that Landy had fielded a team to dress as exterminators and pay a call on Constance Young. What did Constance Young mean to the Union? Apparently not a damn thing. If what she'd told me was the truth, Rathjen still had no idea she was trying to crack his inner circle with her Hackel-forged love lyrics. No, wait, that wasn't right. They'd killed Hackel, so they must know he'd forged the verses for her, so they must know who she was. But that wasn't right either. Hackel had been dead two to three months and the Union hadn't made a move against the woman in all that time. So why make this move against me tonight? Ah, that must be it! The brothers reported the Killabug scam to Dextraze, and he of all people would recognize the name of Constance Young because he'd tried to force her into his first scheme to grab the Kilby estate, ten years ago. That would explain why the brothers had been sent after me.

But in that case I wouldn't be the only target. Had they found Landy already or was he underground, dodging another Drakean goon squad? What had they done to Constance? Where had they begun shadowing me, at her house this morning or the parking garage this afternoon or the Airhotel earlier this evening? The Lynx purred through the deserted cobblestoned streets of downtown and swung west onto the Great River Road while a troop of unanswerable questions paraded in my head. I touched my earlobe gently with a fingertip and felt nothing.

"You ever talk to dead people?" Orvis asked.

The Lynx hummed west, parallel with the river. Barge lamps gleamed through the screen of trees. Tug horns hooted at the new lock and dam, where tiny figures scurried in the wash of light, raising and lowering the gates.

"I do," he said. "Done it since I was a kid when my folks took me to wakes. I used to wonder what the dead knew that I didn't. Used to go up to the coffins and ask them. When I got older and my daddy took Fencl and me hunting, I'd talk to the dead deer. Kids do weird things."

The river slid past on our left and the bluffs on our right. Light from a vest-pocket shopping center bathed the Lynx for an instant and fell away behind us into the dark. A slice of moon grinned down on the earth wickedly.

"Took me till I was fifteen before I saw what I was doing wrong. Didn't do no good talking to animals or people *after* they're dead. Gotta get to them just *before* they die, that's when you learn something. I wish I could have been a prison chaplain back when they had a lot of electrocutions."

We passed the spot where the Piasa bird perched on a cliff overhead like a vulture waiting for its meat. The Lynx cut speed, took its place in a crawling line of cars, brake lights glowing along the highway like a jumble of rubies.

"That's the reason I'm a Drakean," he said. "I get to talk with people just before they die. Like you, friend."

I could feel myself beginning to shake. More than anything else I was afraid I'd lose control of my bladder muscles. I made myself pinch my scorched ear. Pain shot through me like an electric current. In a crazy way I felt better, as ready as I'd ever be to carry on a conversation with this maniac next to me.

"I don't mind talking with you," I said. "Do you mind answering a few questions for me? There are things I'd like to know, too."

He grinned quietly in the darkness. Took out a toothpick and began working it against the edge of his gums. "That's a new one for me, Fencl," he remarked. "Guy has questions for me."

"He don't believe he's dead yet," Fencl grunted. "Hey, Orvis, what the fuck's this jam-up about?"

"Lecture tonight. Some old geezer giving a talk about Barnabas Drake at the university library. Hey, you saw the signs, brother." He snapped the toothpick in half and tossed the pieces out the side window, treated me to another of those slow country-boy grins. "I'd surely love to listen to that talk, friend. If you die quick enough maybe I can."

"I'd still like to ask you those questions," I said, "as long as we're stuck in traffic." I didn't give him a chance to say no. "For instance, what happened to the black guy? The one who played the foreman of the exterminators?"

"You care about the jigaboo, do you?"

"I just want to know what happened to him."

"Well, I want you *not* to know. Makes you worry more."

The Lynx inched forward along the highway. Halfway up the next stretch of straight road I could see where the cars were turning inward toward the bluffs. At the arched entrance gate to Barnabas Drake University. There wasn't any doubt that we were headed there too. If Union Island had been our destination, Fencl would have veered out into the left lane long ago and bypassed the traffic snarl.

"Any more questions?" Orvis asked.

They would have been a waste of breath. I leaned back and tried to concentrate on the loveliness of the night. The Lynx turned right at the BDU gateway and climbed the steep winding road that led to the top of the bluffs. Guards in billed caps and glow-in-the-dark bibs waved the line of cars on with sweeps of their flashlight beams. The road straightened out and cut through stands of birch and oak, with the bluff edge only yards away. In the far distance the lights of St. Louis made a grayish haze along the skyline. A guard tried to herd the Lynx into a parking lot the size of a football field. Fencl opened the driver's window and said a few words I couldn't hear. The guard waved us on. Clusters of brick buildings aglow with light sailed past us. Dormitories, I guessed. We began to pass knots of young people bundled in sweaters and windbreakers against the night chill, books and notepads under their arms. The road led past tall massive stone buildings I guessed were devoted to classrooms and administration, then past a long low squat structure which, judging from the gym bags people were taking in and out of the front doors, must be the rec center. Ahead of us, bright as a wedding cake under floodlights, was the stately edifice of steel and stone and glass toward which a line of pedestrians was streaming. Fencl swung the Lynx off the road onto an access path that led to a tiny paved square at the rear of the library marked *Deliveries Only* and braked and clicked off the headlights.

"Do we wait till the crowd's inside?" Fencl half-turned in the driver's seat and ignited another filter tip.

"No need," Orvis told him. "We belong."

Fencl got out of the Lynx and locked the driver's door and came around and unlocked the passenger door and motioned me out. I squirmed past the pushed-forward back of the front passenger seat, and Fencl kept me under the eye of his .38 while his brother followed me out. They positioned themselves one on each side of me and we started to march toward the floodlit main entrance of the library. Right into the thin steady stream of men and women—young and middle-aged and old, smartly dressed and casually dressed and dressed in the clothes of poverty, white and black and Hispanic and Oriental—converging on the steel-framed bank of doors. I was going to be tortured and killed in that place, and all I could think of was that mad moment in Hitchcock's *North by Northwest* when Cary Grant is being taken down to his death by two hit men in a crowded elevator and he tries to tell the other people in the cage that these guys are going to kill him and everyone laughs. I didn't think the reaction of this crowd would be any different if I were to shoot my mouth off on the way to the library. Hell, these were Drakeans too, they'd probably help Orvis and Fencl cut me open.

We passed through the doors into the great rotunda, which was egg-shaped and marble-walled and open to the skylight five stories above. Velvet rope barriers and well-groomed attendants channelized the entering herd across the center of the rotunda with the Drakean oval sculpted into the flooring and along one of the six passageways that branched out from the open space. At the end of the corridor I saw the doors of the auditorium, flung wide and flanked by security guards in uniforms of Drakean blue-gray and royal purple. Another brace of guards sat at attention in front of a table with a portable plug-in phone on it. Fencl and Orvis and I between them turned off before we reached the doors, into a narrow side passage. The three sentries at the passage mouth didn't so much as blink when we went by. To them we were invisible. We cast grotesque shadows that flowed along the dimly lit walls beside us. Fencl reached into his pocket for a tiny cylindrical key, which he thrust into a slot next to a door in the wall. The door slid back for us. We went down a cramped staircase and through another door that seemed to work on the same key and along more corridors. I tried to memorize landmarks so that, if I got lucky, I'd know my way back and out. Two lefts, a right, past an array of egg sculptures mounted on a wall, another left, and we were standing in front of a steel double door on whose forbidding surface hung the inscription *Barnabas Drake Manuscript and Artifact Collection: No Admittance*.

So this was the end of the trail, the Drakean holy of holies. Orvis took a plastic card from his wallet and inserted it into a slot beside the door. At first nothing happened, and we stood there motionless like worshippers at a shrine. Then the doors made clicking noises and came open and the brothers and I stepped in. A barrel-chested young black man in Drakean guard regalia stood stiffly beside an oval mahogany table littered with newspapers and the remains of a roast beef and cheese sandwich. At the edge of the table a Mr. Coffee unit was plugged into the wall. The room was egg-shaped and low-ceilinged, with white protuberances like gigantic nipples stuck into the ceiling tiles every few feet. I guessed they were heat sensors for the fire protection system. What the system protected was arranged on tall shelves protruding from the curved walls. Row upon row of polished hand-carved sandalwood boxes, each one double-locked and steel-reinforced and harboring one of the multitudinous manuscripts of Barnabas Drake. Scattered through the room were egg-shaped glass display cases, each carefully labeled; one holding Drake's pipes, another his shaving mug, the largest enclosing the silver saddle on which he rode in patriotic parades. The walls were lined with ancient photographs, some of old Barnabas alone, some of him in conclave with other celebs of his time, with Ulysses S. Grant and Teddy Roosevelt and Henry James and Mark Twain and Pope Leo XIII and Oliver Wendell Holmes and Richard Wagner. A huge framed map showed the expansion of Drake's railroads before The Event. Orvis and Fencl let me wander around the room as if they wanted me to share their pride in the man to whose vision they were committed. When I looked back at the entranceway I saw that the black guard was gone.

The next time I looked at the entranceway, perhaps five minutes later, the guard was back but he wasn't alone. He had brought with him a white man of about forty, of medium height, plump-hipped, dark-haired, ferret-faced, sharp-nosed and with an air of humming tautness and cold calculation in every movement he made.

"Whoever you are," he said, "you don't look like much."

That voice! I had heard it all too many times on the radio while staking out 5407 Sturges Place. The man in the doorway was Dr. Mark Dextraze, doctrinal colinory of the university community, voluant ferio of the Circle, heir apparent to the centrality of the Union, studying me with bright pale eyes as if I were a worm he'd encountered in his breakfast apple. I looked back at him with what I believe and hope was cool contemptuous objectivity, while my instincts absorbed his face and figure and ran with them to a place where reason could not follow and *yes, yes, yes,* my voice screamed at me in the silence of the vault, and I knew all there was to know.

"Very soon now," Dextraze said softly, "you'll look different. I want you to think about what razor blades imbedded in a baseball bat will do to your face."

"Is that a threat, Squeaky?" I demanded. Imprudent words to be sure, but I was preoccupied with my sudden discovery of the answer and with trying not to let my knowledge show, and the stupid insult escaped me.

Orvis stabbed out with his foot and caught me in the groin before I could dodge, and I yelped and doubled over into a womb of pain. The brothers grabbed my arms and dragged me to my knees as Dextraze slowly advanced on us. In a split second all my defenses melted away, and I was quivering in the arms of the brothers and howling with helplessness and rage and pain, and Dextraze was standing before me cold as death. That was when I became Sarah Rogers, knowing every nuance of terror she had known the night the brothers and Rathjen had visited her. I felt vomit rising in my throat. Any moment now Dextraze would unzip his fly.

Only he didn't. All he did was look at his wristwatch.

"Later," he said tonelessly. "Doctor Mastrezat's lecture is about to begin." He stepped back from me as if I were a putrefying corpse. "Make him afraid," he told the brothers. "Then bring him to the offering room and prepare him. I shall return at ten-thirty. When I see him again I want him to be without his lips and teeth."

"Sir!" Orvis cleared his throat embarrassedly. "Sir, if it's okay with you I'd like very much to hear the lecture. My brother can handle this for a while. I'll come back soon as the talk's over and help with the razors and the pliers in the offering room."

Dextraze squinted his eyes shut, then opened them wide. "If you wish," he said. "Come then, you will sit at my side."

"See you, friend," Orvis said to me, and let go my arm and marched out of the vault three steps behind his master. The double doors clicked shut after them, and I was alone in that oval shrine with an illiterate sociopath and with the pain slicing through me.

Fencl took a few steps back. I fell over on my side with my eyes still streaming and lay there panting hoarsely. The worst of the pain was receding, but I exerted every ounce of thespic ability I had left to make sure Fencl didn't find that out. As long as he thought I was suffering the agonies of the damned he probably wouldn't bother doing anything more to me, but if once he thought I could take more punishment he'd be only too ready to dish it out. So I lay there curled in the fetal position and howled out my pain and, as the real pain faded, let my mind go to work on getting out of this nightmare.

But my mind refused to function. A few minutes' leeway at best, and I was too paralyzed by terror to be able to think.

Until darling Fencl did something that handed me what

I needed all garnished and tied up in tinsel like a Christmas gift.

He looked down at me retching in more than half-pretended agony and reached into his pocket and fished out a filter tip and stuck it between his lips and reached for his Bic and stopped. Shook his head sadly, pocketed his lighter, and took the dry cigarette out of his mouth and set it on the mahogany table behind him.

That was what gave it to me. The most priceless gift I'd ever been given. My own life back. But it was a gift of the now-or-never variety. Deprived by objective conditions of one pleasure, he'd be in the mood now to substitute another, kicking me in the balls again, or maybe cutting me.

I made myself lurch to my feet. Propped myself against a hand-rubbed mahogany bookcase full of Barnabas Drake first editions. Tried to psych myself with every trick of the mind I knew.

"You stupid fucking sack of shit," I said. "You still have no idea what this is all about, do you?"

He looked at me through eyes slitted like the eyes of a hunter with an eight-point buck in his rifle sights. "You like to hurt, huh, man? I'll make you hurt good. This is a holy place. This is a good place to do things to you." He reached into his shoulder holster for his .38. "Maybe in the kneecaps would be nice."

"You let me talk for sixty seconds," I told him, "then you can kneecap me if you still want to." I didn't give him time to think about it. "Remember all those credit cards and driver's licenses and things your brother found in my wallet? Remember that some of them were in the name of Arthur Lattman, the private cop?"

"Yeah," he said. "Sort of. So who gives a shit?"

"I am Arthur Lattman, you fuckhead!" I screamed at him. "Don't you ever read the papers, watch TV? I run one of the best-known PI outfits in the country! I am working for your pope, your guru, whatever you call him. Rathjen!"

The look on his face was the quintessence of stupidity, but at least some of the sadistic light in his eyes was gone.

"You're too dumb to know it," I said, "but there's a power struggle going on right now for control of this religion. Rathjen thinks Dextraze doesn't want to wait any longer to become the head cheese. He thinks there's a coup in the works."

"What the fuck's a coo?" Fencl asked.

I cursed myself for using a big word like that on him. "He thinks Dextraze is planning to kill him and take over," I explained with the patience of a father trying to communicate with an idiot child. "Just like in the old gangster movies. You've seen gangster movies, haven't you?"

"I don't like that kind of picture," he said. "Too violent."

"But you know what I'm talking about, right? Look, Rathjen has had a couple of suspicious accidents over the last year. He thinks Dextraze rigged them to get rid of him. He came to me secretly and paid me half a million bucks to investigate and report back to him. I've been on the case for months. I had information that this Constance Young woman may have been involved with Dextraze. The black guy that hired you and your brother works for me. That exterminator scam was to get me into Young's house so I could search the place last night. And I found the evidence! She's in on the conspiracy with Dextraze. They're going to try and kill Rathjen again soon, maybe even tonight. And he's sitting in that auditorium right now, probably with Dextraze in the next seat!"

Now the look on his face was one of awe-stricken

incomprehension. He moved his lips as if he were saying something, but no sounds came out.

"Your brother said he was a good Drakean," I said. "Are you? Are you loyal to Rathjen or are you part of the gang that's trying to kill him? I'm betting my life you're loyal to the true center of the Circle. If I'm wrong," I said, taking perhaps the largest gamble of the Milonian career, "then shoot me now." The pain in my groin was forgotten, my blood roared, I kept my eyes fixed on his, blazing at him, willing him to believe me, willing him not to shoot.

He didn't.

"Shit," he said. "I've been a Drakean longer than my brother. I brought him into the Circle." He still looked frustrated and baffled but nowhere near convinced, but the .38 was pointed at the floor now, not at me. "Oh, shit, I don't know what to do now," he mumbled.

"I'm not asking you to take me on blind faith," I told him. "Listen, Fencl. Rathjen is upstairs right now, in that auditorium listening to the lecture, right? There are guards with him and guards at the doors, right? There's a telephone at the guards' station, right?" I pointed to the oval desk at right angles to the vault doors. "And there's a phone in here too. *Use it!* Call the guards upstairs, tell them to bring Rathjen down here on the double, it's an emergency. Use my name. Have them tell him Mr. Lattman has the information for him. That's all you have to do. You and Orvis are going to be heroes for helping break the plot against the unity of the Circle. Promotions, decorations, whatever your religion does to give special thanks to people. Every minute counts. Make the call."

Power beyond myself must have been with me that night. Slow as though wading through neck-deep water, Fencl edged backward toward the reception desk, eyes still baffled and struggling. I straightened and moved slowly across the vault, coming closer and closer but never too close, circling him till I was at the wall a foot from the edge of the desk, while he stood across the oval barrier from me with his eyes darting from me to the phone to me again.

At last they settled on the phone. He scooped up the handset and started to tap a number.

The instant his eyes left me, I did it.

Lunged for the silex pot sitting in the Mr. Coffee unit and flung the boiling black stuff into his stupid face. He yowled. The phone banged to the floor. He pawed his eyes and screeched and I vaulted the desk and something Landy had said flashed into my memory and I kicked him square in the left kneecap and he winced and I kicked him square in the right kneecap and that was the busted one and he shrieked even louder and rolled and writhed on the floor in a cocoon of agony.

What was left in the coffee maker I hurled at one of the white plastic nipples bedded in the ceiling tiles. The heat sensors. Alarm gongs burst and there were hissing sounds like fifty teakettles aboil and a soft white cloud poured down over the vault. Carbon dioxide. Deadliest fire protection system in the world. Kill any living thing in thirty to sixty seconds but leaves a fire no oxygen to feed on. The way to go if you prefer paper products to lives.

I tossed the empty coffeepot into the center of the vault and ran for the double doors and I tripped over Fencl howling on the floor and felt hands locking on my ankle like a steel trap and teeth raking my calf. I kicked and stamped the way I had on the roach and I felt his face crack and go squishy under my shoes and heard retching gagging sounds that muffled his screams and dove away from his mouth before he vomited pieces of himself over me. I dropped to my knees and groped through his pockets as he writhed and bucked on the floor, and I felt a key container and a wallet and plucked them out and held them close to my eyes and just made out through the cloud of gas that the keys were his and the wallet was mine. Then I pawed him for his gun and took that too. He wasn't rolling around anymore, just lying still and mewling like a kitten. I crawled through the filmy curtain of CO2 to where I thought the doors were and ordered myself not to breathe and banged up against something that felt cold and hard and explored its surface with my hands. Steel! The doors! Dextraze and Orvis and the guard had gotten out just by turning the handle. Where the fuck was the handle? I ran my hands up and down the invisible surface of the steel doors and found it. Tugged, pushed, pulled, did everything but tear it out of its socket while Fencl's low mewling died away in the fog behind me. Years later, it opened. I was out, into the corridor, into the light. Out here the alarm bells screamed twice as loud. I pulled the door shut, stumbled to my feet. Guards came running down the corridor from one end. I tore along the same corridor but the other way, sprinting blindly, frantically hunting for any of the landmarks I'd noted on the way in. There, there on the wall, an egg sculpture. The same one I'd seen before? Couldn't tell for sure. The alarm siren flooded the corridors but no more guards came. Everyone but a skeleton force seemed to be at the lecture. I had to find the way back to the main library. Two lefts and a right, wasn't it, before we'd passed the egg? I made a left at the next turning, then two rights. Eureka! The door. Or at least a door. I stabbed the hole beside it with the cylindrical key from Fencl's pocket and the door slid back. As it slid shut again I heard footsteps pounding down the corridor I'd just vacated. The cramped staircase rose ahead of me into the upper reaches. I climbed. At the top, the other door that worked on Fencl's key. I used it and went through. No alarm up here, everything calm and empty, the long dimly lit corridor on which our shadows had flowed pointing like an arrow towards the side passage that came out at right angles to the auditorium. I stayed rooted there at the far end of the passage, breathing, listening, waiting, releasing the safety on Fencl's .38. The first six people to come down the passage toward me, men, women, children, anybody, were going to get bullets in the face. No one came. I couldn't understand it. Why weren't the alarms going off in here? Then I did understand it. The separate underground structure that housed the vault and the labyrinth of corridors and the offering room, whatever that unspeakable place was, had only one connection with the main library building, namely the sliding door whose cylindrical key was entrusted only to the elect. By now the security guards posted at the auditorium doors must have been reached by phone, must have been told of the disaster in the holy of holies. Why hadn't pandemonium broken loose up here?

When I was sufficiently bored by the confines of the side corridor I made my way toward the mouth of the passageway with all the stealth I could muster, my shadow oozing along the wall beside me. At the juncture with the major corridor I risked poking a slice of my head around the corner to see how many guards I'd have to contend with. The answer was zero. The double doors were wide open and the space around the doorway was jammed with people, standing rapt and with heads cocked forward toward the auditorium as if desperate not to miss a word of the speaker inside. Several of those people wore the blue-and-purple guard uniforms, but they too were facing inward and blithely unaware of anything amiss in the corridor behind them. The herd of standees had shoved back the table where the guards had been sitting. I saw the flexcord of the plug-in security phone trailing limply on the marble floor like a dead snake. No wonder the vault crew couldn't get through to the auditorium guards! The god of luck was with me. All I had to do was step out into the main corridor, follow it back to the rotunda, make it out into the open, and start running.

The microphone system inside the auditorium carried the oration past the entranced mob in the doorway and out into the side corridor, where I was still lurking. ". . . not a self-contained center of being, no, that is not at all Barnabas Drake's vision of the egg. A symmetrical body throbbing, pulsing with the life of the entity at its center, giving of its life to the totality of being!"

I had been hearing that cracked, wheezy, vibrant, and compelling voice for at least three minutes, but it was only now that I recognized it, and when I did my feet almost went out from under me. It was the voice I had first heard, God, how many weeks ago, in my own high-rise condo on Central Park South. The unmistakable voice of Ewan P. McGaughy.

And I had gone through that ordeal in the vault fortified by the knowledge that I understood everything that was going on around me. Some satori.

I knew it was McGaughy but I still couldn't believe it. I had to edge closer, see into the auditorium, catch a glimpse of him at the podium. I tiptoed across the dozen feet of open space that separated the side corridor from the outer reaches of the spillover crowd and merged into the blob of devotees. Not a single one of them paid any attention to me. I was as invisible as the last strap-hanger who elbows his way into the center car of a New York subway at five in the afternoon. I strained to see past the blue-and-purple shoulders of the guard who stood immediately in front of me without pushing or shoving or doing anything to call attention to myself. I could make out three men seated on the edge of the auditorium's stage. Knowing what I did of the way guest speakers are introduced, I figured one of the trio had to be Dr. Rathjen. The speaker at the lighted podium was too short, I couldn't get a clear glimpse of him thanks to the blockage of my line of sight by a hundred or more standees. But that voice, discoursing rapturously about the true inwardness of the Drakean religious perception, that voice could belong to no one on this earth but McGaughy. What the hell was he doing here? Why had he set up an alternate identity as Mastrezat? Why was he lecturing on theological arcana at Barnabas Drake University?

This was no place to speculate on such questions. I had to get out of here, find a phone and call Constance Young and warn her, if it wasn't already too late, that she might be visited at any moment. I had to find Landy, if they hadn't killed him yet. I made myself stay right where I was. Now that I had blended into this Drakean mass I couldn't unblend myself inconspicuously. I had no choice but to stand there and wait for the disquisition to end and then slip out in the midst of the fifteen hundred flaming fanatics who would be surging out of the auditorium.

So I stood quietly in the corridor and listened to McGaughy spinning out his doctrinal subleties and looked attentive and counted the seconds and prayed for him to be done.

And at last he stopped, and a storm of applause filled the auditorium, and the seated listeners rose to their feet as one person and their clapping boomed like cannon fire. It was a standing ovation more spirited than I had ever heard at the symphony or the opera. Impatience may have skewed my perception of the time span, but it seemed to go on for hours. Finally the mob seated itself again, and a tall powerful white-haired figure rose from one of the armchairs at the left rear of the stage and came forward to the microphone. Even at that distance I recognized him as Rathjen. He made a mercifully brief speech of thanks to Mastrezat and thanked the audience for coming and he pronounced on the assemblage some gobbledygook I took for a Drakean blessing and bid his followers good evening. The crowd dutifully waited until he and McGaughy and the rest of the party on the stage had left by a rear exit before the exodus began. I flung myself into the outgoing tide of bodies and let myself be carried by the human wave along the main corridor and across the central rotunda and through the bank of front doors and out into the crisp cool kiss of the night.

I felt like part of a lemming migration, keeping to the same pace as the army of Drakeans all around me, moving along the paved walkway that connected this part of the campus with the visitor parking lot. When we came off the path and plunged into the steel sea of cars, the mob disintegrated into a chaotic assortment of individuals, and I scurried out of the mainstream and found the road the brothers and I had come in on and followed it to the deliveries bay at the rear of the library. The Lynx still sat there lonely in the moonlight. The key ring I had taken from Fencl got me inside it. There wasn't a sign of disturbance anywhere around the library. I swung the Lynx into the main road, braked where the legion of visitor cars were merging into the traffic pattern. Inch by painful inch the line of cars crawled down the steep curved road to the arched entrance gates and the juncture with the river highway. The thirty-seven minutes it took me to make it from the top of the hill to the guard post at the bottom crawled by like thirty-seven years. The guards waved each car into the highway with sweeps of their flashlight beams. Not a single auto was stopped or even given a second look. When it was my turn to swing out into the highway I flicked on my turn signal, kept my eyes straight ahead, waited for the bright sweep of the guard's flash, and hung a left. And then I was humming smoothly along the public road, free and safe and breathing. I unleashed a whoop of primal joy and let go of the steering wheel and, for one terrible moment before I woke to reality and grabbed it again, I thought the Lynx and I were going to run off the road into the river.

It was a few minutes past eleven when I swerved across the highway into the parking lot of the dinky little shopping center tucked against the foot of the bluffs. The only place with its lights still blazing was a convenience store. I cut the Lynx's headbeams and went in. There was a plastic-hooded pay phone inside the doorway. I dropped a quarter into the slot and tapped out Constance's number. The blonde woman behind the cash register eyed me warily. The ringing went on and on in my ear. No one picked up at the other end. That was when I knew they'd gotten her too. The two of them were dead or being tortured, Constance and Landy both, and I was helpless. I banged down the phone and went back to the Lynx and tore down the highway into Monckton and along the boulevard to the residential district. At the turnoff to Sturges Place I slowed to a legal speed, cruised past several blocks of bulky dimly lit houses till I was abreast of 5407. In which not a light was showing. I braked, loped to the door, leaned on the bell for a full two minutes. No light came on, nothing stirred. If she was in there she was dead. I didn't dare break in and look because the burglar alarm system would bring me unwanted company before I could fairly get started. I didn't even dare stand out in the cold pressing the doorbell any longer because any neighbor who spotted me might put in a 911 call at any moment. I left the Lynx where it stood and jogged the few blocks to the not-so-safe house on Hunter Drive and ungaraged the Camry with the suitcase still in its trunk and streaked through the midnight emptiness of the interstate and found a slot in the parking field behind the ghostly cylinder of the Airhotel. As I cut the headlights I saw that its tank was almost empty. So was mine. Exhausted, bewildered, frustrated, lost, guilty, and alone, I trundled the suitcase full of equipment through the vast deserted lobby and into a transparent cage that slid up the side of the building and released me on my floor. Running on automatic pilot, I found the door to 1808, slipped my card into the slot, and stepped into the dark doorway and groped for the light switch.

Something exploded out of the dark and landed on me. An arm strong as a crowbar circled my neck in a choke hold. I kicked out at whoever it was like a mule, flailed out with my hands, hoping to ruin his face, his eyes. I missed him but hit the light switch. The room hall flooded with light. The arm around my neck was brown. I twisted my head and saw his face and it was long and bright-eyed and lantern-jawed with a close-cropped mustache and beard. He saw my face at the same moment and let loose his stranglehold.

"Shit!" he grunted solemnly. "You scared the pants off me, man, I thought you was from the Union."

"I thought you were dead," I croaked. Gingerly I felt where my neck had been. Nothing seemed broken, but I knew I'd have to wear a scarf for a few weeks to hide the bruises. "How the hell did you get in here?"

"Found where they keep the cards the maids use to get in," he said. "Borrowed one."

I shouldered past him to the dresser, where I kept the bourbon bottle and poured three fingers into a water glass. "Why didn't you stay in your own room?"

"It's occupied," he said.

The implication in that remark took a few moments to penetrate to my thought center, but when it did I felt a wild crazy elation that, with no help from the whiskey, made me tingle all over. "Do I read you right? You brought someone with you who's in seven-forty-three right now?"

"You got it," he said.

"Mrs. Young?"

"Right on," he said.

"Landy," I told him, taking another gulp of bourbon in celebration, "you've just made my night. Now start explaining."

I listened to most of his story as I stretched out in the bathtub, submerged to the chin in steaming water, a glassful of neat bourbon tottering on the ridged soap shelf. At the end of the Killabug show at the Young house, he had driven the van and the crew back to the parking garage that had been the staging area for the operation, had paid off the help, returned the van, and picked up his own car, returning to the Airhotel to clean up and get normal again. Last night, while I had been shivering in Constance's basement and imagining roaches crawling up my bod, he had enjoyed a fine dinner with wine, topped off with more booze than was good for him. Around noon today, feeling sober enough to handle a car and curious whether my mission had been a success, he had driven back to the riverfront parking garage to see if the Camry was still berthed there. What did he find as he approached the garage? The two brothers from the Killabug job—white siblings, that is, not black men—sitting in a Mercury Lynx half a block from the place and across the street. It looked to him like a stakeout. Two other whites in a second car, a Chevy Caprice, seemed to be on the job with them. The setup didn't look cool to Landy, so he commenced to watch the watchers. Around two-thirty all five of them had observed Mrs. Young dropping me off in her car. The pair in the Caprice had taken off after her, and the pair in the Lynx after me and the Camry. Landy had opted to follow the Caprice. With the two shadow cars in her wake, Constance had gone back to 5407 Sturges Place and put her wheels away. The Caprice pair had driven off to a pay phone, made a call, them come back and staked out the Young house.

"They acted like they was about to make a move on her," he said as I climbed out of the tub and toweled myself. "Right after it got dark, they did. Rang her bell, said they was police, stuck guns in her face when she opened up."

"Sounds like you were right on top of them when it happened."

"Right on their dumb asses," he agreed. "They got the drop on her and I got the drop on them."

"What happened?"

"I killed them," he said. "They in her basement now. They was about to do it to her."

"Good for you," I said. I sheathed myself in pajamas and robe and crawled between the bedcovers, yawning like a chasm.

"Then I told Miz Young she better pack some things and come out here with me. I put her in my room cause I figured it was safer."

"What happened to Jim Socks?" I asked. "The cat?"

"Neighbor's takin' care of the cat for her till the trouble's over. Now, man, what's been happenin' with you all this while?"

I was far too tired to narrate my evening's adventures with the detail they deserved, but I hit the high spots, fueled at intervals by refills from the bourbon bottle. Landy sat lotus-style at the foot of the bed, eyes fever-bright as I talked. When I reached the part about the guest speaker at BDU being none other than McGaughy, I watched his face, wanting to see if the revelation would surprise him. If it did I was too far gone to notice.

"Okay," I said at the conclusion of my recital. "Your turn at bat again. Tell me about McGaughy's double life."

"Why does anybody have more than one life?" he countered. "Why you have a bunch of 'em?"

"Are you telling me this is all news to you? I thought you and Kilby were closer to him than anyone in the world."

"We was," he said. "But Mac, he always been a strange dude." He shut up for a minute, narrowed his eyes as if struggling with a decision. "He was a priest once," he said.

That revelation definitely surprised me. Had I not been in bed at the time, I would say that it floored me. I jolted up, punched pillows under my shoulders to prop myself against the headboard. "A priest?" I repeated. "Catholic priest?"

"Yeah, man," he muttered slowly. I think he already regretted having, so to speak, let the Roman collar out of the bag. "Long time ago."

"Why did they kick him out? Booze? Sex?"

"Man, you don't know Mac at all, do you?" he said. "He hardly never takes a drink, and I never saw no sign he had a sex life. I don't understand all this religion stuff, but I think Mac got some ideas in his head that the boss priests didn't think was worth shit, and they told him to give up his ideas or they'd send him to hell or somethin', and he got pissed off and took a walk."

"And then some time after all that happened he met Mr. Kilby, right?"

"He met Mr. Kilby and saved Mr. Kilby," Landy said. "That was one sad dude, man, till Mac done come into his life."

"How do you know that? Did Mac tell you?"

"Mr. Kilby told me," he said. "Us two come from like two different planets, man, but Mac was like a second father to both of us, so I guess that made us like brothers. We used to talk about him. We both used to wish he'd been our real father and raised us."

"You didn't meet Mac till several years after he met Kilby, then?"

"Five years ago I met him." He squeezed his eyes shut again, debating whether to let something else out of the bag. "I tried to mug him one night," he said, "that was how I met him. I was still on horse then, and I needed a shot so bad I was ready to kill for the money. I mugged him. And look what he did for me in return. I'm the only son he got left, and he eighty years old now, he too old to have another."

"How about his connection with the Drakeans? Suppose, when they try this will contest, he gets on the stand and says there's no mystery at all about Kilby leaving everything to the Union, because McGaughy was bending Kilby's ear for months about what a noble religion the Union was?"

"I told you," he said, "I don't understand the religious stuff. But I know whatever he doing with those dudes on the island, he got a good reason."

There's no arguing with love. I stifled another yawn, and saw to my consternation that by the digital clock on the night table it was well past two in the morning. "Sack-out time," I muttered. "Big day coming up."

"Meaning which?"

"We're getting out of here after breakfast," I told him. "You and me and Mrs. Young. Nothing to keep us here any longer."

I set the snooze alarm for 8:00 A.M. and shrouded myself in a cocoon of blankets against the night chill. By ten in the morning, Landy and Constance and I were fed, packed, checked out of the Airhotel and headed north and east in the Camry. Landy drove the first shift while I pored through the Monckton *Conservator*. The story of Dr. Mastrezat's lecture at BDU was featured on page three. Buried in the back pages was a tiny squib about the accidental malfunctioning of the fire alarm system in the Drake manuscript archive. Not a word about the dead man in the vault. Either those Drakeans were cover-up artists of the first water, or they owned the newspaper. Probably both.

Traffic was light on Interstates 40 and 57. By cocktail time I had briefed Constance on last night's developments—except of course for the contents of my satori, which I was sharing with no one—and we were dropping off the Camry at the car rental station beneath O'Hare International Airport. With Landy's Omnitron credit card we purchased three one-way tickets from Chicago to LaGuardia. The east bound flight was smooth as a sheet of glass. We touched down a little after eight in the evening, local time. I phoned the night manager of New York Security from the baggage claim area and arranged for Constance to get an unobtrusive hotel room and round-the-clock protection till further notice.

The evening's last train from Penn Station to Princeton Junction included among its weary passengers Landy and myself. A cab dropped us at Omnitron's headquarters tower just three minutes before midnight. We flung our bags into the suite on the top floor to which Landy had the key, the one that Kilby had used when he was alive, and fell into the twin beds and conked out. My earlobe still throbbed.

9

Although you send for the tender calf amid many cows, it has unerring skill to seek out its own mother. Deeds of old days have even so the power to search him out to whom their fruit pertains.

The Naladiyar

WHEN I WOKE up and rolled over, warily opening one eye and finding the bedroom drenched in cheery sunlight, I had a sneaking suspicion that I'd overslept. The night-table clock read ten minutes to noon. The other bed was crisply made like a bunk in a basic-training barracks, and Landy was gone. A quick look in the front room told me that the suitcases he'd plunked down beside mine last night had dematerialized with him. He hadn't even left me a note. I showered, shaved, dressed, helped myself to juice and Danish from the refrigerator in the suite's compact kitchen, found WQXR on the dial of the TV-radio console in the front room, sat in a wing chair, and basked in the melody of one of the *Bachianas Brasilieras* of Villa-Lobos and tried to put my head together.

Noises from the outside corridor broke into my trance. Pad of shoes on carpet. Soft scrape that sounded very much like a suitcase being leaned against a wall. I went to the entrance door of my own suite and flung it open and there he stood, with his back to me, facing the opposite door until he heard me behind him and swung around. His eyes were unfocused, his parchment cheeks stubbly. He looked used up.

"Sign your book for me, Doctor Mastrezat?" I greeted him.

The words brought a semblance of life back into his eyes. If he was upset that I'd found out his secret name, he didn't show it. I even thought there was a glint of satisfaction in his look.

"Aha," he cackled softly. "Yes, of course, you were there when I gave my little talk at BDU, weren't you? I did think you might be out in that sea of faces. I rather hoped you were." A spasm of coughing cut him off and almost doubled him up. "Brought a bug back with me," he gasped between coughs. "Hope I didn't pass it to Dave."

"Landy was with you just now?"

"Picked me up at Newark Airport this morning. I called him here very late last night. Obviously you slept straight through the call or you wouldn't be looking so surprised. He's gone back to his own place now to catch up on his sleep. Well, I'm sure you're bursting with curiosity about me, even though you're concealing it remarkably well, and I suppose you deserve an explanation." He tapped a code signal into the green square on the wall. The door opposite mine emitted a series of clicks and McGaughy turned the knob. "Will you come into my little parlor?" I picked up his ancient suitcase and followed him inside.

Into a single vast room, easily twenty-five feet square. Every inch of wall space except what went for windows and doorways was given over to bookshelves, great mahogany monsters stretching most of the way to the ceiling, every one of them packed thickly with books and bound periodicals and piles of papers. Half the room was set up as a study, with a table desk and typewriter and file cabinets and more books and papers sprawled every which way across every flat surface. The rest of McGaughy's life was lived in the other half. A few nondescript chairs and tables, a plaid-upholstered couch that I assumed opened out into a bed. The checkerboard parquet was adorned by only one rug, a thick blue shag with a single large egg design imprinted in its center.

I wandered across the room to one bookcase that somehow seemed more orderly than the others. A quick look showed me why. Every volume on its shelves was uniformly bound in blue morocco with pages trimmed in gold leaf. There were no titles on the books' spines, only numbers, ranging from 1 to 72. I gingerly tugged Volume 24 out from its place and opened to the title page. *The Fourth Discourse on The Power Of The Circle In The Life of The World*, it read, and at the bottom of the page the name *Barnabas Drake*. A few more random glances and I saw that what reposed on those shelves was a complete library of old Barnabas's works, the 72 mind-boggling theological-metaphysical-philosophical-cosmological tomes that the erstwhile robber baron had cranked out in the less than fifteen years between The Event and his death.

When I looked up from my find, McGaughy was gone. I heard the roar of running bathwater. Considering the old fox more than capable of trying to pull a fast one on me, I pounded on the locked john door and yelled his name over the thunder of the shower until I got his attention. "What?" he croaked at me through the water and the heavy door between us.

"Nothing!" I shouted back, and went over to one of the shabby armchairs in the living-room area and composed my soul in patience. Unless he was the beneficiary of supernatural powers, there was no way he could slip past me.

Twenty minutes later, scrubbed and shaven and wearing a thick black robe over pajamas, he came out into the front room and lowered himself with a sigh into the chair that was twin to my own. "Coffee?" he smiled. "Wine? Something stronger perhaps?"

"Just an explanation will do," I said. "Or maybe confession would be a better word for it. What do you think, Father?"

"Oh," he said. "So you know that too?" He shrugged nonchalantly as if having once been a priest was a prank of his vanished youth. "Well, as the man said, that was a long time ago in a galaxy far away."

"And you told me you didn't have a religious bone in your body," I said.

"Oh, but my dear Mr. Turner, it's hardly a matter of bones!" he said.

"You're not a Catholic anymore?"

"I probably never was."

"Believe in God?"

"The question is unanswerable."

"But you believe in—" I waved toward the bookshelf that held the collected works of Barnabas Drake, "—in that shit?"

"I believe that Barnabas Drake experienced something," he replied with lawyerly precision. "I believe that The Event was not a hallucination or a hoax."

"And after you met Charles Kilby and became his, well, his confidant," I said, "you played priest again, didn't you? Made up your mind to convert him to the true faith?"

"I did not," he said quietly.

"But you did have his ear? You could influence him more or less as you pleased?"

"I was closer to him than anyone in the world," he said. "But I never tried to suggest what he should believe or how he should live or how he should run his company."

"But you and he talked a lot, right?"
"Sometimes."
"Here in this suite?"
"Sometimes."
"So he must have known how you felt about Drake?"
"I don't know," he said. "I honestly don't know."
"And you knew he'd been having bad problems with his heart?"
"I did know that," he admitted.
"Then it's just a wild coincidence that in the last moments before he died on that Lear jet he seems to have written a holographic will leaving everything he owned to the Drakean Union. Right?"
"I don't know what it is!" A furious light danced in his pale blue eyes. Intensity crackled in his voice. "From the moment it happened I haven't understood it! But I never once in my life suggested anything to him about how he should leave his property. My God, Turner, he was like my son!"
"His first will left half his property to you," I reminded him.
"Yes," he said. "Think about that for a moment. Would I have induced him to revoke that will, cut me out completely and leave everything to the Union?"
"If you believed strongly enough in the Union," I said, "you just might have."
"And would I have arranged for you to come into the picture and fight off the Union? Would I have entered the Drakean camp under a different identity? Wouldn't I have gone to Rathjen and offered my testimony that Chuck had become an ardent Drakean under my tutelage? It must have occurred to you, Mr. Turner, that to this day the other side has never publicly offered an explanation as to *why* Chuck left them everything in that second will. All they can do is speculate on how he *might*

have converted. If I were on their side, they would have done much better than that."

It took a few minutes for me to say anything. I sat there in the creaky armchair and stared into space, trying to make sense out of what defied sense. In the end, all I could say was what McGaughy had said already. "I don't understand it," I said. "I thought I saw it all but . . . " And then I shut up, and we sat there in a frozen silence together.

Which was broken only when McGaughy made a request of me that failed to connect with anything in our dialogue. "Mr. Turner," he said, "tell me what you know of me."

I still have not the foggiest notion why I bothered to answer. Certainly my response did not represent me at my brightest. "Your name is Ewan McGaughy. You used to be a priest. My guess is you belonged to one of the brainier orders, maybe the Jesuits. You got too interested in Drakean study and they kicked you out of the priesthood. You became more and more obsessed with the stuff. You set up a new identity as Dr. Mastrezat, wrote a big book about Barnabas Drake, and got it published by the house that does all the Drakean literature. Then you were invited around to lecture about your ideas. You even got to give talks in the Union's back yard. Meanwhile you had your other life here as the mysterious little imp that had Charles Kilby's ear and kept him more or less on track, and—I don't know if this is the right word—reformed Dave Landy after he mugged you one night in the New York subway."

"Very good," he said. "But don't you know who I am?"

I stared at him blank-faced as an idiot.

"When was I born?" he asked me.

My memory reached back to something Landy had

said not too long ago, about Mac being eighty now and too old to have another son. "1905?" I guessed.

"And when," he asked, "did Barnabas Drake die?"

For that one I had to grope several weeks further back, to our conversation over seafood pasta salad and Pouilly Fuissé in the limo along the Jersey Turnpike, on our way to this tower in which we sat. "That was in 1905 too," I ventured, "wasn't it?"

"Do you know the hour and minute of his death?"

"Of course I don't."

"I do," he said. "It was recorded faithfully by those who were with him at the end." The madman's glow in his eyes intensified to a kind of spirit fire. "It was the hour and minute at which I was born."

The words struck me like a hammer blow full in the face, and finally I understood. This daffy old man believed he was the living reincarnation of Barnabas Drake! Sitting two feet away from a full-fledged religious maniac was a new experience in my life. I didn't try to stand up and walk out of the room because I knew I couldn't move from this spot. I couldn't reason with the man or argue with him. On his own theory, Barnabas Drake must have been living simultaneously as a fetus in McGaughy's mother's womb and in his original body during its last nine months of life. But it would have done no good to point this discrepancy out to him. Every religion in the history of the world has demanded belief in something or other just as ridiculous, and whatever it is has been believed.

"What I created has gone astray," he said softly. "It was known from the beginning that what I would create would go astray. I was sent back to set it right. I've known for years, dozens of years, that this was why I was here, but I didn't know how it was to come about. And I grew older, and older, and—then there was

Charles Kilby. He came into my life, and I thought it was meant. I was afraid. My faith was weak. If I were to die, someone would have to carry on this mission. I thought it was to be he. But he was blind, like you. I loved him but he was blind to everything I said and tried to do. And then . . . then he died, and there was the second will, and Genetelli vanished. *And I knew!*" His voice filled the room with ancient power. No man that old and feeble could have such a voice. "I knew that his death was meant, that everything about his death was meant, that the moment was at hand. That was why I set out to find one who would help the moment be born. That one, Mr. Turner, was you. Your part in all this is meant."

"My part?"

"To destroy!" he said. "To uproot the monstrosities and perversions that gorge on what I created, so that I can begin again!"

"To destroy the Drakean Union?"

"Yes!"

"My God," I said, and sat there as if turned to stone, my mind whirling chaotically in the dark. *He couldn't know*. He couldn't possibly have known that I'd been dreaming and fantasizing about carving the Union into shreds ever since the night Sarah Rogers told me what they did to her. He couldn't know of my talk with Constance Young through the hours till dawn, of my encounter with the enforcement arm of the Union a few hundred yards from where he was passionately discoursing in the BDU auditorium. And most surely of all he couldn't know of the satori I had experienced in room 1808 of the Monckton Airhotel, he couldn't know that even as we spoke I held the Union in the palm of my hand. How could he know? But he did.

I wanted to walk away from all of it. Abort the jihad, run back to New York, be George Boyd again, go to the symphony, make love to a woman. But I wanted even more to kill that sick disgusting religion. And most of all I wanted to kill this bizarre being who had been manipulating me from the beginning, making me want to do what he knew I was meant to do. He scared the life out of me. He came from somewhere else.

"Accept it," he said softly. "It is meant, you know."

I spent the next three days weaving a web. The executive suite across from McGaughy's eyrie became my isolation tank. When I was hungry, that ancient gnome tapped on my door and fixed me a meal. When I was thirsty, he brought me wine. When I ran out of clean duds, he took away with him every item of clothing I had packed for my trip to Monckton and brought them back freshly laundered a few hours later. The one thing he never did was say a word to me.

On the third day I re-entered the world. As business hours got underway I passed through the blank door that cut off the residence block from the rest of the top floor of the Omnitron building and wandered through labyrinthine corridors till I found the file-crammed cubicle within which labored Professor Aaron Donovan. He was buried under a mountain of blue-backed legal documents. When I invited him to take a break from whatever he was doing and play assistant PI for a bit, his eyes lit up behind his Groucho glasses and his teeth flashed in a grin. Fifteen minutes later, with the slender personnel file on Martin Genetelli in his lap and the phone at his ear, he was putting in calls to various members of the faculty of Marquette University Law School with whom he had at least a nodding acquaintance. The process took most of an hour, which I spent sitting across the desk from him, listening to his end of the dialogue, hoping, hoping. At the end of his final call he dropped the handset into its nest and tenderly massaged his red ear.

"Three out of five," he said. "They all remember him more or less the same way. Heavy-set, quiet, brilliant. A few years older than his classmates. Sort of a loner. Kept near the top of his class but never seemed to need to study much. One of his professors indeed referred to him as a born student."

"Good," I said. "That's what I expected."

His eyebrows lifted in a Grouchoesque gesture of confusion. "There's no doubt he went to Marquette," he told me, "if that's what you're interested in. My lord, don't you think the people here would have checked him out before they brought him into the legal department?"

"Up to a point," I said. "Now, how would you like to play assistant detective some more?"

"I'm ready for anything that takes me away from this for a while." He flung his hand about to indicate the document prison around him.

"Indeed?" I said. "Then I've got a chore for you this afternoon. In Jersey City."

The late hours of the morning I devoted to running up long-distance charges on the phone in my own suite. Most of the calls were to people I knew in New York Security, trying to find the right person for the starring role in a little drama I was casting. Having put out feelers, I next made a call in-house, to Colonel Shaw's office. The magic of the Lattman name propelled me through the thicket of secretaries and assistants, and within three minutes the grandee himself was on the line.

"You don't know how badly I want to talk to you," he growled. "McGaughy told me you were back but said you couldn't be disturbed. What the hell went down in Monckton?"

"Long story," I said. "Let's take a meeting over it, shall we? Very privately."

"Where are you?"

"Still in suite D."

"That's as private as we can get. I'll have lunch sent in for the two of us. One o'clock."

"It's a date," I said.

At ten minutes to the appointed hour I opened the suite door to a smiling Oriental in a white mess jacket who trailed in his wake a wheeled cart adorned with silverware, table linen, an ice bucket, and a covered tureen from which came forth an aroma worth killing for. "Turtle soup," the server announced. He set the dining table in the suite, poured sherry into delicate long-stemmed glasses, glanced at his watch, and motioned for me to be seated and stood in the open doorway and gave a little bow as, at one on the dot, Shaw came striding through. Over the kingly repast I filled the colonel in on perhaps fifty percent of the events along the muddy Mississippi. I didn't mention McGaughy's alter ego as a Drakean savant and I didn't go into the details about what I'd learned and what I was planning, but I did make it clear that I had brought home the bacon.

"No ifs, ands, or buts," I said. "No ambiguities, no equivocations. The Union will never take over this company."

Shaw tapped his pipestem against the edge of his water glass, a thin tinkly sound that made my teeth chatter. His eyes kept wandering around the suite, his jaw muscles bunched. He looked like a man who has had to dine on toadstools and poison ivy.

"You haven't been roosting here for three days because you like the scenery," he said. "You're cooking something up."

"Smart man," I said.

"I want to know what."

"You're paying me," I agreed. "You have the right."

He grunted and refilled his pipe from a sealskin tobacco pouch, graciously giving me time to arrange my thoughts.

"There are two ways we can handle the situation," I said. "Option one. I tell you what I've got. You tell your lawyers. The battle in the courts keeps going on for months. Motions, cross-motions, appeals, objections, adjournments. Hundreds of thousands in unnecessary legal expenses. You'll win eventually, but—" I paused for a sip of wine, groping for *le mot juste*—"but not in any telling way," I finished. "Undramatically. That's option one."

"What's the other option?"

"You trust me," I said. "You tell your people to trust me and do what I ask them, and a couple of weeks from now we'll have Rathjen and his gang where they'll never be able to hurt anyone again."

"Lattman, you're demented," he thundered. "I don't give a damn what the Drakean Union does or did as long as they don't get their hands on this company. I'm not trying to put them out of business."

"I am," I said.

"You're going way beyond what we hired you for. I will not let you drag this company into a cockeyed holy war!"

"Yes, you will," I predicted quietly. Pause for effect and a sip of wine. "Because it's the only way you can keep your part in the plot from coming out." And, leaning back expansively in my dining chair, I explained to him precisely what he had done and why he had done it, and watched with a sort of sadistic satisfaction the way the color of his face turned from the gray of weathered stone to the dead grayish white of the dottle of his own pipe to the blank pasty white of a fish's belly. The recital took me but a few minutes. Then I shut up and finished the rest of my soup. He sat there with his lips mashed together and his eyes lost in quiet horror. I think he saw his life crumbling. After a time he blinked like a mole emerging into sunlight and focused on me again.

"Anyone else in the world," he said, "would be shaking me down for everything I owned."

"Probably," I agreed.

"I'd be willing to pay you something," he said.

"If I forgot about the Union and walked away?"

"Far away."

"I won't take a cent from you," I said. "No more than what we agreed on already. I will take your cooperation."

"I could have you killed," he said.

"You could *try* to have me killed," I corrected. "And let's suppose your hit man got lucky. What would you have gained? Just another blackmailer instead of me. Maybe not so ethical a blackmailer as myself."

He sat there giving a passable imitation of a zombie. Present in body only. Eyes squinched shut. Once I thought I saw him shudder.

"I know what I'm doing," I said softly.

And then he took a long breath like a drowning man suddenly thrust up into the oxygen, and I knew he'd made his decision.

"Do it," he said.

I reached my hand across the remnants of our lunch and we shook on the deal. "Shaw," I told him, "they didn't make you a colonel for nothing."

The word went out through conventional corporate channels. From Shaw to La Verne Nixon-Markson, from her to her opposite number at the silk-stocking firm in L.A. that for this purpose was representing the Drakean Union, and in due course from the L.A. firm to the grand high exalted toads of the Union and back along the chain of communication to Shaw, who in turn slipped the answer to me, seven working days after the ball had started rolling. Question from Omnitron: Would the top echelon of the Union and their counsel be interested in a very private meeting with their counterparts on the other side, to be held at Omnitron headquarters, all expenses to be paid by Omnitron, for the purpose of discussing a possible settlement of the litigation over Kilby's wills and a possible transfer of power from Omnitron's present management to the chosen managers of the Union? Answer from the Union: Yes.

Just the answer I had been counting on. Indeed I had been operating during those seven working days—making phone calls, meeting with various technicians here in Jersey and with other people in New York, making commitments of one sort or another—as if I had known in advance that Yes would be the answer. I hated to contemplate the possibilities if the Union had said No.

By mutual arrangement the date and time were set. A Tuesday morning, at 10:00 A.M. sharp. Two days before Thanksgiving. If I had had any doubts that Rathjen himself would be in the visiting party, they dissolved on Monday afternoon when a half-dozen big granite-faced men in dark suits showed up at the ground-floor reception lobby of the Omnitron building and presented credentials as Drakean security people and demanded to check out the area. The receptionist passed the word to Shaw's secretary, who told Shaw, who told me. "Let them," I said, and whooshed out a private sigh of relief. The big guns of the Union were definitely going to be in the group. Lawyers didn't rate such protection. Omnitron's chief of security gave the Drakeans a tour of the parts of the building that would be used the next day, and after three hours of futzing around, the six from nowhere pronounced themselves satisfied and vanished. Their black Cadillac gunned out of the company parking lot at a few minutes after six in the evening. Nine hundred and fifty minutes before zero hour.

Somewhere around four in the morning, I gave up trying to sleep. Dressing in the dark, I took my keyed-up nerves for a walk, through the empty corridors to the tiny spiral staircase that led to the bullet-shaped plastic bubble on Omnitron's roof. There I stood again, surrounded by the night, cool and clear and bright with the twinkling of uncountable stars. I remembered McGaughy standing beside me in the bubble, reciting lines from Kilby's poem about the symphony of light. I felt at one with the ghosts of Beethoven, Bruckner, Mahler, Shostakovich, for I had devoted every waking moment of the past weeks to orchestrating a symphony of my own, and its world premiere was six hours away, and I had the jitters. I tried to let the night soothe me. Didn't help. Too much might go wrong come morning. One sour note and the audience for which my little composition was intended might literally massacre me.

Long before dawn I was back in suite D, fueled on strong coffee, jumpy as a kangaroo. Nothing happened. Nothing was supposed to happen. I watched the grayish morning light drift in through the windows and counted the seconds as the readout on my digital watch crept infinitesimally toward ten.

At precisely 9:52 by its taillight-red figures, the phone shrieked. I grabbed it in mid-ring. "What?" I growled.

"They here." It was Landy, calling from somewhere on the ground floor, my link with the action for the next three hours. "They just clocked in at Reception."

"How many?"

"Four stretch limos full. Most of them be lawyers or guns."

"Rathjen there?"

"You bet. He come marching in like Napoleon or Hitler."

"And Dextraze? Foxy-faced one with the plump butt?"

"He with them."

"Oh frabjous day! Calloo callay!" I said.

"Huh?"

"Nothing," I said. "Keep in touch, but for God's sake stay out of sight, okay?" I checked my readout again. "Our people should begin showing up in another half hour. You're sure you know where they go?"

"We sure been over it enough," he sighed.

"Call me as they check in."

"Anything else, man?"

I was about to suggest teasingly that he pray but decided he might take it literally and said a simple No and hung up.

Over the next three hours he called me fourteen times with a quickie news flash. Like: "Bunch of guys wearin' monkey suits under their raincoats just checkin' in." Or: "TV and newspaper people beginnin' to show up for the press conference." The conference was scheduled for the employees' garden, the one on the east side of the building, and had been called to announce completion of work on a new 1.5 micron microprocessor chip. Poring through Omnitron's development reports and finding the right subject for a press conference had kept me up two nights running. Or: "The fat man's in." That was the message I most wanted to hear.

The last call came at 12:57 P.M. "Colonel just passed me word in the john," Landy announced. "Meeting's just breakin' up. They takin' the elevator down to the big shots' garden for lunch."

"Did he say how the discussions went?"

"He said they done wasted the morning on bullshit like you told him you wanted."

"Okay," I told him. "Go for your hole and make sure you're not seen."

"I'm black and I'm dressed like a waiter," he said. "Who's to see me?"

"And send McGaughy up here now."

"He just left."

The old ferret and I intersected in the doorway of suite D. His gummy eyes were brighter and his crease-strewn face more alive with joy than I'd ever seen them before. We clasped each other's hands on the run as he passed in and I passed out. I took the fire stairs down to the executive garden.

Which had been transformed by my blueprint into the setting for a business lunch.

The hanging plants and ferns were all in place, but the wrought-iron tables were gone and with them the ambience of a sidewalk cafe. The artificial waterfall was silent and dry, no placid rushing sound to compete with conversation. Two long tables curved symmetrically down the center of the vast room like an inside-out parenthesis, one wing for Omnitroners and the other for Drakeans, prandial mingling strictly forbidden. Twenty-two places had been set on Omnitron's side. Shaw dined at the center of his curved table, flanked by carrot-thatched Fest and stuttering Vanderwell, with La Verne Nixon-Markson on Fest's left and an owlishly blinking Professor Donovan exiled to the extreme far end. The others on that side were unfamiliar to me but had to be either lawyers or department heads. On the Drakean side of the parenthesis there were sixteen diners, with Rathjen lordly and straight-backed at the center space opposite the colonel, and several ponderous types with lawyer written all over them flanking the high ferio and Dextraze four spots to the head cheese's right. The beefy members of the group, the security men, were at the ends of the Drakean table, all except three who stood at intervals between the table and the plant-screened window wall, eyes hooded and wary. A corps of waiters and waitresses in mess jackets kept on the hop between the diners' tables and a serving area and portable bar near the elevator, bearing highballs, wine carafes, chafing dishes abulge with crab Rangoon, water pitchers, Caesar salads, prime rib entrees, urns of steaming coffee. The vast room resounded with cutlery clatter and chatter buzz. In my rented tux I wandered about the garden, giving, if I do say so myself, a more than passable imitation of a food service supervisor, pausing now and then to whisper a discreet admonition to a waitress or busboy. Unobtrusively I scanned the faces of Rathjen's gun crew. My old friend Orvis wasn't among them. I wondered what he'd said to the mashed corpse of his brother. The only one in the gang who might prematurely recognize me and hit the alarm bell was Dextraze, and he had seen me only for a minute. For safety's sake I kept my back to the Drakeans as much as I dared and also kept on the go, exchanging vague nods with the dozen Omnitron security guards in standard issue uniforms, who prowled lackadaisically through the garden, munching crab Rangoon. Lunch wended its way without incident from appetizer to dessert like Robin Hood without his merry men. As the legion of servers came charging across the room with wedges of cannoli pie, I made my move.

To the locked fire door at the end of the garden farthest from the elevator.

I used the key on it and pulled it open and the man who'd been waiting for two hours in the darkness of the stairwell stepped out behind me into the dazzling light of the garden. A plump squat man of medium height, with crisp dark hair and a heavy coating of five o'clock shadow, encased in a suit too tight for him, sweat sheen on his forehead. He carried a battery microphone in each hand. The one in his left hand he tossed to me. We were on our marks within nine seconds of the time I'd unlocked the door. Two of the three standing gunmen were eyeing us curiously by then, but that was all.

"It's show time!" I announced into the mike. "Servers, move back!"

With Rockette precision the waiters and waitresses scurried away from the Omnitron table and the Drakean table and formed tense little groups in the room space between the service area and the dining area.

"Most business lunches have a guest speaker," I said. "Our guest today is a person whom many of us have wanted to hear for a long time." I made a half-turn toward the fat-farm candidate standing three feet from me. "Ladies and gentlemen, Mr. Martin Genetelli."

No applause greeted my introduction, but the stunned silence that enveloped the garden in less than fifteen seconds was precisely the response I wanted. Cups clattered down in saucers, chair legs scraped as diners on either side of the parenthesis maneuvered for a better view, but not the whisper of a human voice was to be heard, only a few nervous coughs. I scanned the faces on the Union side. They ranged the gamut from blankness to seething anger to utter bewilderment. Rathjen's looked frozen but emotionless, his eyes veiled, looking down at his hands as they rested one atop the other on the tablecloth. Dextraze was staring at the two of us as if any moment his eyeballs might pop out and roll along the floor like marbles. His jaw muscles and Adam's apple writhed furiously. Surprise had caught him midway through a bite of pie, and his mouth had gone so dry he couldn't get the chunk down. I tried very hard not to laugh.

"Thank you, Mr. Lattman," the chubby one croaked. "And thanks also for tracking me down. You're a damn fine detective, sir." To which compliment, inserted in the script by myself, I responded with a modest nod and a smile.

"This speech," he began, "is in the nature of a confession. As most of you know, I was, except for the pilot, of course, who was in the cockpit at the time, the only person in the company Lear jet with Charles Kilby when he died. Shortly after the holographic will he allegedly executed in his last moments was handed over to the police, I went underground. Some people thought I'd been murdered. Well, I may get killed later on today but it hasn't happened yet." He let out a small edgy giggle.

"When I joined the legal department here at Omnitron," he went on, "I had a—I guess you'd call it a hidden agenda. The job for its own sake meant nothing. What I really wanted was proximity to Mr. Kilby, and I didn't care how long it took to get it. You see, I had a dream. My dream was to forge Mr. Kilby's signature to a will I was going to prepare, a will that would leave everything he owned, and particularly his huge block of stock in this corporation, to what was then my religion. The Drakean Union."

The silence at the dining tables gave way to a low rumble of voices. I kept my eyes on the two key faces. Rathjen's dead as stone, Dextraze's falling apart. The Drakean guards who were on their feet shifted restlessly as if they needed to visit the john.

"A few months after coming aboard here I made a proposal to a corporate officer whose help I felt I needed. The proposal was that I would prepare a will, a straightforward typewritten will, in which Mr. Kilby would make a few routine charitable bequests for appearances' sake but would divide the vast bulk of his property into two equal parts, with half to go to the Drakean Union and the other half to my, er, new partner. He and I would sign this will as witnesses, and after Mr. Kilby's death we'd testify that he executed the will in front of us. I did prepare such a will, complete except of course for the signature. Then we sat back and waited for the right opportunity to—well, to murder Mr. Kilby. That was the plan as I proposed it to this person."

My attention had shifted across the garden to the Omnitron side of the table, and the ashen-faced horripilated reaction on the face of one particular person made my heart pound with pleasure. Keeping my eyes on that face, I spoke into the mike. "Did you intend to carry out the plan as you proposed it?"

"Not completely, sir," he said. "My real plan was to forge a will in which Mr. Kilby would leave *everything* to the Drakean Union. The kind of will that doesn't require witnesses, a holographic will. The proposal I made to the other person was a ruse, to get his cooperation. I would have the will forged leaving him half, we'd hide it among Mr. Kilby's private papers, and in due course we'd—well, murder him."

"And this other person agreed to work with you?"

"Yes, he did."

"Mr. Genetelli," I asked, "who was that other person?"

He took a few seconds to answer. I kept my eyes on the face at the center of the Omnitron table. It was staring at me with a fury and a terror beyond my power to describe. First Genetelli had tricked him into a conspiracy to commit murder, and then I had mousetrapped him into helping me expose himself, and now he was looking at his own ruination only microseconds away and he couldn't do a damn thing to stop it. He seemed to be willing me to burst into flames and melt.

"How do you think I got to be head of the legal department so quickly?" the plump one demanded rhetorically. "It was Colonel Shaw."

The quiet rumble mounted to a roar. Fest and Vanderwell flinched, backed their chairs away from Shaw's central position as if it were a plague spot. Shaw didn't move a muscle, just sat there transfixed.

"Go on, Mr. Genetelli," I urged. "Tell us your real plan."

"Well, even before I came to work here I knew that Mr. Kilby spent much of his time in California. As a lawyer I knew that California is one of the few large states that still recognizes holographic wills. Soon after joining this company's legal department I heard about Mr. Kilby's bad heart. That was when I decided that I might not have to commit murder to carry out my plan, that it would be less risky to wait and see if nature would do the dirty work for me."

"So your revised plan was to forge a holographic will and wait for Kilby to die?"

"That's correct."

"But you're not a forger yourself, are you?"

"Oh, no, sir." Another edgy giggle. "They didn't teach us that in law school."

"Then how did you go about obtaining a forged will?"

"It wasn't all that difficult." He smiled mischievously, licked his lips with a fat strawberry tongue. "The Drakean Union has certain underworld connections. I was able to use them to find out who were the best document forgers in the country. The person I settled on was a man in San Francisco named Hackel. I paid Mr. Hackel thirty thousand dollars to forge a holographic will, more or less extrapolating the handwriting from the few available specimens of Mr. Kilby's signature."

"And did he in fact forge that will for you?"

"Yes, he did."

The garden was dead silent again, everyone including the waiters and waitresses and the uniformed Omnitron guards straining forward to catch every word as if the fate of the world depended on it.

"And gave it to you?"

"Yes."

"And what did you do with it?"

"Nothing," he said. "I kept it with me at all times while I waited and hoped and prayed—Drakeans do pray, you know—for Mr. Kilby to drop dead."

"You didn't plant it among Kilby's papers?"

"Not then. I was afraid to. If I planted it too soon, he

or someone else might have found it, and that would have been—" He halted as if stuck for the right word.

"Embarrassing?" I suggested.

"Precisely," he agreed. "I did substitute the Cross pen Mr. Hackel used in the forgery for the one Mr. Kilby habitually carried with him, and I kept the forged will close by me at all times. If and when Mr. Kilby died, I'd have to be among the first to know, and I could then add an appropriate date to the will—just in numerals so there wouldn't be any handwriting discrepancies—and secrete the document among his papers. That was my plan."

"And then, as luck would have it, you were on the Lear jet and alone with Kilby when he did have his heart attack?"

"I didn't see it as luck," he corrected. "I saw it as *meant*."

"And you had the forged will on you in the plane when he died?"

"Yes, sir."

"So you sat there in the lounge of that jet and watched him die and didn't lift a finger to try and save him?"

"It was meant," he repeated, with not a trace of remorse.

"And then?"

"I used the pen in his pocket, which was the one Mr. Hackel had used in the forgery, to add the numerals of that day's date at the top of the sheet of paper. I put the sheet in an Omnitron envelope from the supply of stationery in the lounge and put the envelope in Mr. Kilby's jacket pocket. Then I mussed myself up a bit and rushed to the cockpit and got the pilot to come back with me and try to administer CPR."

"But you knew Mr. Kilby was already dead?"

"Yes."

"And you went into hiding not long afterward. Why did you do that?"

His eyes shifted to the Omnitron side of the garden. "Because I was afraid, when he found out how I'd fooled him, Colonel Shaw would send hit men after me. I knew I'd have to come forward eventually and give depositions and testify in the will contest, but I decided to stay underground until the last possible moment."

"And while you were in hiding you began to have second thoughts, is that it?"

"All sorts of second thoughts," he said. "About a lot of things. I . . . er . . . saw a priest, asked him to hear my confession. I wanted to come back to the Catholic church. This was, oh, maybe a month before you found me, Mr. Lattman."

The script wasn't working right. The room was dead silent again, Rathjen was still staring cool and poker-faced into a distance no one else could see. Dextraze had his swallowing apparatus in gear but otherwise wasn't reacting. Shaw was still a study in stone. *Come on, one of you bastards, do something!* I kept up the dialogue only a minute or two longer before ringing down the curtain.

"Thanks for your help, Mr. Genetelli," I said. "Now, ladies and gentlemen, no doubt you're wondering how I could have been so sure that the alleged Kilby holographic will was a forgery. That too is an interesting story, and I've brought someone along to tell it." With that I strode confidently to the unlocked fire door and tugged it open. "Your turn," I said into the stairwell. Constance Young flashed me a stage-frightened smile and came out into the garden behind me.

"This," I said to the audience, "is Mrs. Constance Young. Mrs. Young, will you please briefly tell us about your dealings with a man in San Francisco named Hackel?"

"Gladly," she said. "I, well, I had reason to need some papers prepared that would seem to be in the handwriting of the late Charles Kilby." She glanced hesitantly over at Dextraze, who was reacting to the latest speaker with something like apoplexy. "Do you want me to go into what my reasons were?"

"Not necessary," I told her. "But they weren't criminal in nature, so we'll leave it at that. The bottom line is, you needed a document forger."

"Yes. And I made some discreet inquiries and found a man in San Francisco named Hackel who was supposed to be very good at that kind of work, and, well, I hired him."

"This was some time after Kilby's death?"

"A couple of months afterward."

"That's a crucial point," I told the listeners in an aside. "Now, without going into too much detail, the documents you had Hackel forge included more than once the word 'will,' is that correct? Not the noun, as in 'last will and testament,' but the verb form, as in 'I will come tomorrow.' Right?"

"Yes," she said softly.

"That," I turned to the audience again, "was the giveaway. Hackel was getting old and lazy, or else he saw an opportunity for a bit of blackmail later on. He had obviously kept some sort of copy of the Kilby will he'd forged for Mr. Genetelli. Now a second person had paid him to forge something that could pass for Kilby's handwriting. This wasn't much of a coincidence; he was one of the best in his business. Anyway, instead of taking the trouble to forge the word 'will' from scratch whenever it appeared in the documents Mrs. Young wanted prepared, Hackel took the easy way and traced the word 'will' as he'd already forged it in the Kilby will for Mr. Genetelli." That revelation did evoke a murmur in the listeners. "I happened to wind up with copies of both the Young forgery and the Genetelli forgery. Once I held one up against the other, the truth hit me in the face." I took another look at Dextraze, to see how he was holding up under the assault. Too well. His ferret eyes were composed again, his features calm and relaxed as if he'd sworn a great oath to the spirit of Barnabas Drake to weather this storm however long it took. Time to turn up the pressure a few more notches.

"Mrs. Young," I said, "tell us about the first contact you ever had with the Drakean Union."

This was the moment she'd been waiting and dreaming and praying and plotting for, the moment when she could ascend a public forum and tell the world the truth about the Union. I watched the nervousness slip from her like a shed skin. Her eyes grew brighter, her stance more erect. She stopped her foot shuffling, stood with feet firmly planted, and reached out for the mike in the hand of the plump young man who had spoken before her. And in a voice sharp and powerful as the knell of doom she told about the day in the spring of 1976 when a ferret-faced little man walked in on her while she was alone in her husband's real estate office in a small town in Iowa, and all the rest of the campaign of subtle terror the little man had waged against her. I paid no attention to her, having heard the tale more than once already, and concentrated on the audience. Were they getting the message? Were they seeing that the pattern of Genetelli's deal with Colonel Shaw at Omnitron was the same as the pattern of the deal Dextraze had proposed to Constance Young more than ten years ago?

They seemed to be. As Constance went on with her story, more and more dubious looks were trained on stoic Rathjen, even some from the lawyers on his own side of the table. He saw those looks. I could see on his face his feeling that the tide had swung against him, that he or Dextraze had to do something, defend themselves somehow then and there. He lifted one finger, gestured to Dextraze to approach him. The lawyer either didn't see the summons or ignored it. Rathjen rose from his chair, stalked behind the three functionaries who sat between him and his protégé, beckoned the one next to Dextraze to vacate his seat. The functionary leapt up as if he'd been goosed. Rathjen dropped into the chair, huddled with Dextraze, got no response, shook him gruffly by the shoulders, got no response. I signaled Constance to keep on talking, stretch out the story. Every hair on the back of my neck told me something would explode if I kept up the pressure. Already the two were acting as if they were alone on a distant island, with no eyes watching their furtive whisperings. Constance's voice droned through the mike. *Come on, you son of a bitch, go for it!* I pleaded silently, as if my thoughts could make him move.

And maybe they could and did, or maybe it was a fluke of timing, but that was precisely when Rathjen got up again and lifted both arms in the air for quiet. I nodded at Constance to stop.

"I will not tolerate this vicious attack on my religion for another moment!" he thundered. They were the first words I had heard up close from the boss ferio's mouth. He spoke with authority. You might well believe he could calm the waves, heal the sick, raise the dead with that voice. "Woman, you have lied against the peace of the Circle. Your suffering will be great. And you!" He pointed his right forefinger with its missing joint at the plump man somewhere near the wall at my back. "You will know pain such as no man has yet known!" He took a dozen steps backward until all the diners on both sides of the garden were in his line of vision. "That man is a liar and an impostor!" he boomed. "That is not Martin Genetelli!"

"How do you know?" I shouted back at him, flinging down the mike I didn't need anymore. He had done it. Now he was a fly sitting in the palm of my hand, waiting

to be squashed. "I'll tell you how you know. It's because the real Martin Genetelli, as far as there ever was one, is sitting at your table right now, calling himself Dextraze. And you've known it all along, and I can prove it!"

Rathjen's mouth moved but it was like the movement of a dummy's mouth. Nothing came out.

"This man beside me is an actor," I explained to the dumbstruck audience. "I had him make up as Genetelli from the photographs in his Omnitron personnel file. Everything he confessed to is true, except for a few details I had to guess at and except when he said he was Genetelli. Rathjen, I staged this little play to psych you and Dextraze out, and by God you fell for it! Your boy over there messed up nine years ago when he tried to make Mrs. Young help him grab Kilby's fortune for the Union. But he didn't quit. He tried the same plan again only with different trimmings. He put on thirty or forty pounds, had his vocal cords altered, had some plastic surgery done on his face, built up a paper identity as Genetelli. I sent Professor Donovan to Jersey City to see if any of the faculty or staff at St. Peter's College remembered him, and no one ever heard of the guy. All of Genetelli's college credentials were fakes. But he couldn't take that kind of chance with law school credentials, which he figured would be more carefully checked. So he went through law school a second time—no wonder he was so bright without having to study!—and graduated, and passed the New Jersey bar, all as Genetelli. Then he came to Omnitron and made his pitch to Shaw, who didn't have Mrs. Young's scruples. With Shaw's help behind the scenes, he got promoted to department head in record time. He saw more and more of Kilby on company business, began traveling around with him on visits to branch offices. As you've heard, he planned all along to doublecross Shaw, and when the time came, he did. Once Kilby was dead, 'Genetelli' disappeared. We know now where he went: back to Monckton, to Union Island. He had the plastic surgery undone, got his vocal cords fixed again, lost a bunch of the weight he'd put on for the part. But your voice wound up squeaking when you get excited, and you couldn't starve all the blubber off your ass, could you, Dextraze? In time he'd probably have to gain some pounds back for his court appearance as Genetelli, but having his weight bounce up and down like a yoyo was a cheap price to pay for a company that nets ninety mil a year. Now do you see how he got to be named the voluant ferio so young?

"In case any of you still doubt what I'm saying, let's have a test." The test was a bluff, but I gambled Dextraze was too shook up to notice. "Genetelli disappeared rather hastily after Kilby's death. One of the little things he forgot to do was to remove all his fingerprints from the house in Penns Neck, where he was living. After he went underground, Omnitron hired a firm of investigators—not mine, unfortunately—to find him. That firm failed, but it did lift a set of his prints from the house, and a copy of that set is in its report. Now, I happen to have brought a fingerprinting kit with me to this lunch. It's behind that door right now." I indicated the fire door through which I had already sprung two surprises on the throng. "Dextraze, if you're not Genetelli and want to prove it once and for all, come forward and give us your prints."

Dextraze was out of his chair now. Clumsily he sidled past the backs of the chairs of the others on his side of the garden, but in the direction of the elevators, not toward me. "Don't let him past!" I shouted at the knot of waiters and waitresses standing in the middle distance—who were not really waitpersons, of course, but part-time actors and part-time sleuths, courtesy of New York Security, just like the plump gentleman who had played Genetelli for me. They formed a cordon across the garden, herding the hapless Dextraze the way range drovers would herd a stray yearling back to the main body of the trail drive. Now he and Rathjen were standing there within a few feet of each other, isolated in the glare of attention, trembling-fingered and shamefaced, like Adam and Eve caught in their nakedness and sin in an earlier garden.

"Colonel Shaw." I turned toward that paragon of the parade ground, who still sat rapt and stunned as if the planet around him had toasted itself in a nuclear holocaust with himself the only survivor. "Would you tell us if the man who calls himself Dextraze is the same man who called himself Genetelli and made a deal with you and left you holding the bag when Kilby died?"

He cleared his throat very softly but the sound had the effect of a shotgun going off. Like a man in a hypnotic trance he jerked to his feet and wove slowly past the others from the Omnitron luncheon party, lurching into the open space where Rathjen and Dextraze were standing. Dextraze stayed rooted there like a rabbit under the eye of a snake as Shaw edged closer and closer.

He didn't even lift his hands to protect himself when Shaw made a leap for his throat.

La Verne Nixon-Markson screamed. Men shoved chairs back, jumped to their feet, shuffled around going nowhere. Three detectives in waiter outfits ran forward and shoved Rathjen aside and piled on top of the brawlers, trying to wrench them apart. Rathjen stumbled back and clawed at the curved table for support and got a fistful of snowy linen in his hand and the edge of the table in the small of his back and fell forward, taking the tablecloth and assorted crockery with him to the floor. His bodyguards were barreling out from behind the long table or vaulting over it to reach the open space and shield their leader, but as each gunman made his move he was tackled by two or three of my waiter-actor-detectives and quickly stripped of his weapon and sent sprawling off to one side with his arms pinioned behind him. The battle was over in less than a minute: Shaw and Dextraze howling and writhing in the arms of the detectives who were keeping them apart, their tongues lolling and eyes popping like patients in the last stages of Huntington's chorea; Rathjen isolated in the middle of the room, struggling pitifully to get up; his enforcers disarmed and helpless; Landy and the troops I'd held in reserve bursting out of their hidey-holes in the fire stairway and roaming the room trying to keep the noncombatants calm. Total victory without a shot being fired.

I marched across the garden to where Rathjen was still down on one knee and held out a hand and jerked him to his feet, squeezing his hand brutally as a vise, wishing I could tear out his fingers by their roots, wishing I could stamp his face into jelly the way I had with Fencl. "It's over," I told him. "Cut your losses."

I almost felt a twinge of sorrow for that disgusting old man as he stood there panting, rubbing one hand with the other, darting panicky glances this way and that, like a deer cornered by a wolf, trying to recover control, frantic to salvage from the debacle whatever he could. Almost but not quite. I backed away a few steps and waited to see if he had the presence of mind to take the line I would have taken in his shoes. He did.

"I . . . knew nothing of this . . . treacherous plot," he gasped, still struggling to bring his breathing back to normal. "I . . . was blind to so much. And that unspeakable traitor—he was to succeed me! Mr. Lattman, you have saved the Circle from being fouled and corrupted. Every Drakean is in your debt." That godlike voice was sending out hypnotic waves again, and it would have been so gloriously easy to let myself go under. I didn't.

"Oh, of course!" I said. "It was Dextraze and his faction that did all the bad stuff! All on their little own.

I'll bet you don't even know what they did to old Hackel in San Francisco, or what they tried to do to me and Mrs. Young back in Monckton."

A passable semblance of surprise formed on his face. "Surely you don't think I knew . . ."

"Do you think Dextraze is going to take the punishment like a good little boy and let you walk away? Look over there." I pointed to the far corner of the Omnitron table, where the voluant ferio was sitting slumped in a chair, his mouth moving a mile a minute, and ready-for-anything Aaron Donovan was bending over to catch every word, a midget cassette recorder dangling from a leather strap in his hand. "But you'll have your chance to play innocent, friend. In fact you'll have it any second now. The media are coming. I had one of Omnitron's departments call a major press conference this morning to announce a technological breakthrough. That conference was going on in the employees' garden on the other side of this building, until twenty minutes ago when I gave a signal from in here. Rathjen, did you ever bother to learn what this company manufactures?" The look on his face was blank and uncomprehending. "One of the things they make is miniaturized video cameras they sell to police departments for surveillance work. There are twelve of them hidden all over this room. When I gave my signal a dozen monitors were lowered from the ceiling in the other garden and all those media people saw and heard everything that just happened in here. You've been a closed-circuit TV star today." I heard the whine of the elevator at the end of the vast room. "Here comes the contingent now. Let's see you kill *this* story."

The elevator door glided back and a herd of news types with conventional-sized video cameras held over their heads scurried into the garden. The cage whispered shut and went up to receive another horde from the media. Rathjen squeezed his eyes closed. I thought I saw a tear trembling along the side of his nose. I wondered if, from his private monitor at the top of the building in suite D, McGaughy could see it too. "It is meant, you know," he had said.

Rathjen straightened and wiped the corners of his eyes, ran a hand through his white mane and expelled a long breath, stepping forward into the center of the open space in the garden. The reporters and cameramen formed a circle around him, or maybe it was an oval. I almost believed he could talk his way out of it.

10

If the Circle shall be weakened, it shall fortify itself and be strong again. If the Circle shall be pierced, it shall mend itself and be whole again. If the Circle shall be fouled, it shall cleanse itself and be pure again. If the Circle shall be torn asunder, it shall heal itself and be whole again. For the center of the Circle cannot be weakened. The center of the Circle cannot be pierced. The center of the Circle cannot be fouled. The center of the Circle cannot be torn asunder. I am the center of the Circle forever. Children of the Unity, hear this in your hearts.

The First Discourse Of Barnabas Drake,
Chapter 14, Exhortation 6

THE LAST TIME I saw McGaughy it was May, one of those treasure days when the sun slips in and out of cotton candy cloud formations in a sky too blue to be real, and when every midtowner with a bit of free time and a soul takes a postlunch constitutional through the walkways of Central Park.

I don't know what the winter had been like in Lamoni, Iowa, where Constance Young had returned with her cat. It had been a mild winter for New Yorkers and a bitter one for the Drakean Union. The events at that luncheon in the garden had splattered across the media like a watermelon dropped from a rooftop. Dextraze had talked a blue streak in front of a small army of microphones and video packs, giving away not only his lunatic scheme to seize Omnitron but an assortment of other outrages in which the Union had figured. On that overcast Tuesday afternoon, everything burst forth that pressure and connections and terrorism had kept suppressed for years. Public diarrhea, some wit dubbed it. The media went goggle-eyed with the intensity of the exposure, unrivaled since the palmy days of Watergate. Hardly a winter evening passed without a new revelation of Drakean infamy on the network news. Rathjen became as indefensible as Nixon. Each time he called a press conference to rebut the latest charges and slam the media for antireligious bias, he looked guiltier than the last time. By February his own cable channel and a few diehards in the newsmagazines were the only supporters he had left. Then the FCC lifted the Drake Cable Network's license for blatant violations of the Fairness Doctrine, and Rathjen's last defenders wrote him off when Sarah Rogers went public with the story of how she'd been raped and fired from *Time*. Federal and state authorities belatedly found all sorts of laws Rathjen and his gang had broken, from tax evasion to mail and wire fraud to conspiracy to commit murder. They never could prove as it would have needed to be proved in court that Rathjen had personally known about the Dextraze plot against Omnitron or had taken part in it directly. They never did connect anyone in the Union with Hackel's murder in San Francisco, and there was always the possibility he'd been wasted by others, for reasons that we'd never know. It hardly mattered. There was no room for more nails in Rathjen's coffin. On the first Friday in April, in his office at the heart of Union Island, he had stuck a .357 Magnum into his mouth and blown his brains onto the wall. Neat trick for a guy missing the top joint of his trigger finger.

And on this sunny May afternoon I was sauntering along the people-clogged walkways of Central Park, carefree as the robins chirping in the bright green branches, when suddenly I felt a tug at my jacket sleeve and there he was. McGaughy, materialized out of nowhere, puffing as if he'd had to run to catch me, flashing me that benevolent loon grin. I grabbed his hand and pumped it warmly and beamed at his wrinkled prune face and his eyes dancing in the sunlight. "It's been a while," I said.

"Too long," he said.

"I didn't feel you needed me anymore."

"Well, you certainly accomplished all we asked you to do and then some! I don't know if you follow the business news, but under the new management team Omnitron's doing better than ever."

"Nice for you," I said. "As owner of half Kilby's stock under his genuine will, you're richer than ever now."

"I suppose so," he said modestly.

"But you still wear that shiny old suit," I told him.

"I'm used to it," he said. "You know, I really expected to hear from you again. Certainly you haven't forgotten the terms of your arrangement with the company? We still owe you half a million dollars."

"I know. That was what Shaw promised me when I finished the job."

"And finish you did, most satisfactorily! The company is bound by his commitment."

"Even after I sandbagged him at that lunch?"

"Especially after that," he said. "You know, I always did wonder how Genetelli rose in the legal department so fast." His rheumy eyes watered in the brightness of the sun. "Dave drove me into town in the limo. I thought that was you I saw crossing over into the park when we turned into Fifty-Ninth. He's circling around for a while.

The money's with him." He paused. "I'm afraid we shan't see each other again. I've sold my shares in Omnitron, and Dave and I are leaving at the end of the week."

"Where are you going?"

"To Union Island," he said. "To the work I was put on earth to complete. McGaughy is dead. Mastrezat lives."

"To take over the Drakean Union?"

"To heal the breach in the Circle. Restore it to what it was meant to be. The false ones are destroyed now, dead or impotent. The wrong and the rot are exposed, some of it at least, and first of all the task of uprooting must be completed. Quiety, subtly, with cunning."

"If you're not careful," I said, as if I cared a damn about the future of that crackpot religion, "you won't have anyone left inside your Circle, you and Landy will be all alone there."

"Many have left already. Many more will go. Those who entered into the Circle through deception, or through fear, or because they were born to parents within the Circle—let them leave and be happy elsewhere. The Circle wants no slaves, only free believers."

"You're talking as if you're already in charge of the Union," I reminded him. "No one's made you the high ferio yet."

"It must be," he said dreamily. "Do you think it just happened that my first son founded a company which the Union tried to possess? Do you think it just happened that you were brought into these events? No. The time had come for the Circle to be torn asunder, and you were my destined blade. Do you think you succeeded because you are so wise and clever? No. You were meant to succeed. All that happened since we first met was . . . orchestrated. A symphony of events. No note was played at random. Now that symphony has entered another movement, which will end when the Circle is pure and whole again as it was the day I first left the earth."

I have never known how to deal with the obsessed. This genial little wizard truly believed he was Barnabas redux, and that belief was beyond shaking. You cannot communicate with these people in their private language and you can't use the language of reason either. But I liked the old man and trusted him—after all, he knew much too much about me but had never once tried to capitalize on it—and so as we cut across a soft green meadow running through the park I made a final effort to reach him.

"McGaughy," I said, "you are eighty years old. Do you honestly expect to live to see the Circle pure again?"

He looked at me, or maybe through me. "I don't know," he said. "I honestly don't. My former life ended when I was eighty-three. This is why I had to prepare one to come after me."

That was when I saw what he saw, and as we stood there among the trees and the rocks and the gaily shrieking children, I was dazzled by something that was not the sun. "Landy," I said.

"My only surviving son," he said softly. "If I'm to die and the work is unfinished, he will bring it to completion."

"He told me flat out he doesn't understand any of your religious talk," I said.

"He only thinks he doesn't understand," McGaughy said.

That amiable beanpole, ex-killer in uniform, ex-doper, ex-street thief, with his halting command of the language and his ache for a woman he could never have, the man who had first met McGaughy when he mugged him in the subway, that man was going to become the leader of something approaching a world-class religion. I couldn't believe it, and one of my voices told me it was inevitable. I remembered the awed and longing look he'd given the concentric oval structures on Union Island, where the heart of the Circle beat. Too much, too much! There was a hollow roaring in my head. I wanted to run and scream.

"You're a good person," McGaughy said, "but blind. You don't know what your life is for. I don't ask you to believe in us or join us but I would be very pleased if you would wish us good luck."

I stood there frozen in the sunlight for a moment, and then I held out my hand, or maybe my hand held itself out or someone or something held it out for me, and he took it and clasped it between his frail old hands, and it was the fullest moment of my life. "Good luck," I heard myself saying softly.

"Thank you," he said. "Come on now. My son is waiting for us."

If you have enjoyed this book and would like to receive details of other Walker mystery titles, please write to: